RUSH
HOUЯ

Volume I V • Reckless

RUSH

HOUR

A Journal of Contemporary Voices

MICHAEL CART, Editor

DELACORTE PRESS

Published by Delacorte Press
an imprint of Random House Children's Books
a division of Random House, Inc., New York

DELACORTE PRESS and colophon are registered trademarks of
Random House, Inc.

www.randomhouse.com/teens
Educators and librarians, for a variety of teaching tools,
visit us at www.randomhouse.com/teachers

ISBN-13: 978-0-385-73034-1 (trade)—ISBN-13: 978-0-385-90184-0
(lib. bdg.)
ISBN-10: 0-385-73034-9 (trade)—ISBN-10: 0-385-90184-4 (lib. bdg.)
ISSN: 1547-0601

The text of this book is set in 12-point Adobe Garamond.

Printed in the United States of America
10 9 8 7 6 5 4 3 2 1
First Edition

Contents

RUSH
HOUЯ

Introduction

"I shall make the reckless choice," poet Robert Frost wrote in "The Sound of Trees."

I love that phrase, "the reckless choice." It sounds so extravagant and wonderfully romantic, doesn't it? Imagine being bold enough to *choose* to act without fearing the consequences. Or at least that's what the words mean to me. And my *American Heritage Dictionary* tends to agree, defining that operative word *reckless* as meaning "indifferent to or disregardful of consequences." But it also means, the dictionary adds, "heedless or careless, headstrong or rash."

I made the reckless choice only once in my otherwise carefully planned and orchestrated life: Thirty-two years ago I quit my secure job as director of my hometown public library in Indiana and moved to Hollywood to try to

become an actor. I had no prospects, only the burning desire to do something different with my life, something—
well—unexpected, unpredictable. If people thought I was
being heedless or careless, headstrong or rash, so be it. I
didn't really care. More important to me than what people
thought was pursuing a creative life, and to me, that meant
a life lived in front of a motion picture camera or onstage in
front of an audience. I was at a crossroads in my life: I was
thirty-two years old and I knew that if I didn't make the
reckless choice then, I probably never would. And so I
heeded the words of yet another Frost poem. You know the
one I mean. "The Road Not Taken," the one with the
haunting lines

> Two roads diverged in a wood, and I—
> I took the one less traveled by,
> And that has made all the difference.

Oh, I never became an actor, but the road I took led me to
my present life, which is filled with another kind of creative
activity: writing books as well as editing, and assembling,
each new issue of *Rush Hour*.

And in *that* context, it's not important what either the
dictionary or I have to say about the meaning of recklessness. What's important is how the seventeen authors and
artists who have contributed to this issue have chosen to
define the word with their work. And, as always, they have
been wonderfully varied in their choices.

The first three entries—the short stories by Greg Galloway and Sharon G. Flake and the photograph by Tabitha

Soren that links them—remind us that even the reckless must deal with the consequences of their actions, though sometimes those consequences may be forced on them by others.

The three poems by Kiwi and the short story by David Levithan that follow examine how very reckless falling in love can make us, since then it's the heedless human heart that does the choosing.

Next, artist Mo Willem's hilarious drawing "Eyepoker" offers both a refreshing change of mood *and* a reminder that sometimes second thoughts about recklessness may be preferable to, well, a poke in the eye.

Then Ben Foster's autobiographical essay and Terry Quinn's poem invite us to consider how our very environment—whether a therapeutic community or urban mean streets—may impose recklessness on us.

Manuel Muñoz's story "The Heart Finds Its Own Conclusion," on the other hand, artfully investigates a situation in which the fallout from a reckless choice unexpectedly affects not the chooser's life but that of an innocent other.

In the interview that follows, Man Booker Prize–winning author Yann Martel muses about an altogether different kind of reckless behavior: the act of writing itself!

The excerpt from Helen Frost's forthcoming novel in poetry, *The Braid,* and Elizabeth Wein's short story "Chain of Events" are linked in several interesting ways: though they take place a century or more apart, both are set in Scotland and both examine reckless behavior by girls in the context of life-changing voyages, one by sea and one by air.

Very different girls are the reckless protagonists of the

next two features: Tommy Kovac's darkly imaginative story in pictures "The New Girl" and Bennett Madison's edgy short story "Little Sisters Steal the Best Shit."

Boys and the sometimes melancholy consequences of reckless behavior (though not always their own) provide the focus of A. M. Jenkins's and Martin Wilson's stories and wind up this issue of *Rush Hour*, which then concludes not with words but with Pascal Lemaitre's whimsical drawings of behavior that takes recklessness just about as far as it can go, and hang the consequences.

Thanks for making the reckless choice to read this issue of *Rush Hour*. Here's hoping you'll enjoy it.

—*Michael Cart*, Editor

Vocabulary

Gregory Galloway

Copse. Jim had never heard of it, and now he had to use it in a sentence. Mr. Gaines always handed out the hard ones on Friday. There was a list on Monday and another on Friday, with the harder words on Friday. That never made sense to him. He thought about asking his father, sitting right there across the table, with his newspaper erected between them. It was a fortress wall, a DO NOT DISTURB sign; his father could not be engaged until the paper had been lowered. It didn't matter; his father wouldn't know what it meant either. He'd have to look it up. He didn't even know if his father owned a dictionary. He could have moved down the list to *dolorous* or *ejectment* or *quandary* or *thrall,* but Jim closed his notebook and put his pen down on the kitchen table and decided to do it later, maybe when he went home on Sunday. There was plenty of time for homework, although he didn't know what else could fill up the time.

His father lowered the paper and looked at him. "Finished your homework?"

"Done."

"You want to read the paper?"

"Not right now." It was his third weekend in a row with his father; he needed a break.

"The newspaper has the news; people don't know what they're missing by just watching it on TV. That's not news. Am I right?"

"Right."

"Right. You want to look at some TV?"

"Whatever." He hated watching television with his father. About the only thing the guy watched anymore were cooking shows. His father couldn't get enough of them; he would watch seven or eight of them in a row, all those different women doing the same thing over and over, cutting and slicing, sprinkling salt and pepper over some hunk of meat and then cutting to commercial and they come back and talk about how great it tastes. It could taste like shit, what would anyone know? They make it all look so easy; he wished his father would try it sometime. He never cooked, but he liked watching the shows; it didn't matter which one.

They moved into the living room and his father took his usual spot in the recliner. Jim brought in the paper and took a seat on the couch. If a cooking show came on, he'd read the paper. The second the TV was on, there was some woman chopping an onion and throwing it in a pan. How many times could he watch that? *Zaftig*. That was one of last week's words. The woman wasn't that; there was little pleasing about her. She might have been zaftig once, but now she was like a building that had settled, thickened into a sturdy but unappealing shape. She minced some garlic and threw it in with the onion. She let that cook for a short time and then poured in some white wine and tarragon, and then scooped in a few tablespoons of lemon juice. His father was crazy for this stuff. She cooked the tarragon and onions and garlic down until almost all of the liquid was gone. Then she placed them in a glass bowl and pushed them around with a wooden spoon until they cooled. She then grabbed some soft butter with her meaty hands and massaged the tarragon and onions and garlic into it. He couldn't take a whole weekend of this. Jim stopped watching and started to read the paper.

The only time it ever seemed that his father was intent on talking to him was when he was trying to read the paper. Here he was always pushing it on him to read it, and then whenever he started, the guy would keep interrupting. He had barely finished the weather forecast in the upper right corner before it started. It had rained most of the day, but it was getting a lot colder tonight. He didn't even get to tomorrow.

"No date?" his father said.

"Nothing. How about you?"

"Not tonight. A couple of bachelors on Valentine's Day. What could be better than that?"

"Yeah."

"What's your mother got going? She got something with what's-his-name?"

"Yeah. They're doing something."

"Why didn't they take you along?"

"I don't know."

"Well, another weekend with the old man. It could be worse."

"Yep."

"They must have done something special for Valentine's Day and all."

"They went down to the lake, I think." He wasn't supposed to tell his father that, but he wanted to see his reaction. It was worth it.

"Sonofabitch," his father said. He stood up out of his recliner and took a step to his left and then one to his right; he wanted to do something, but he had no idea what it was. He went into the kitchen and turned on the faucet.

From the couch in the living room Jim could hear the water running, but he couldn't imagine what his father was doing in the kitchen. Soaking his head maybe. He wanted to get up and go look, but that would only aggravate his father. Jim tried to concentrate on the paper, but his attention kept moving back to the running water in the kitchen. The water finally stopped after a few minutes and his father returned to the living room, standing near the end of the couch.

"She said they were going to the lake?"

"Yeah," Jim said, not looking up from the newspaper.

His father went back to the sink. The water ran again. It was still running when his father came back once more.

"With the boyfriend? For the weekend?"

"That's what she said."

"That's what she said? I say, no way. It's not right, I say. No way."

The water stopped and Jim could hear his father foraging in the kitchen, opening drawers and cupboards, pushing boxes and cans and utensils around, shoving stuff around, slamming things shut.

His father returned to the living room wearing his dark brown winter coat and a baseball cap pulled tight over his forehead. He had a small black duffel bag slung across his chest. It looked like a cheap bag, something they give away with magazine subscriptions, but it didn't have a logo on it or anything. He couldn't believe his father would have spent money on it.

"You want to do something fun?"

"Like what?" Jim said.

"Like getting even with your mother."

"I don't need to get even with her."

"How about her boyfriend, then?"

Jim shrugged his shoulders.

"All right. Well, I'm going to have some fun. You can just come along for the ride."

Jim put on his coat and followed his father to the car. It was a lot colder out, with the wind whipping down the street. His father placed the duffel bag between them and idled the engine for a few minutes, waiting for the car to warm up.

Impetus. His father drove south out of town. He drove in silence and after a while unzipped the duffel bag and brought out a bottle of whiskey. His father took a drink of the whiskey and placed the bottle between his legs. He kept his eyes on the road.

"What's he like?" his father asked.

"Who's that?"

"The boyfriend."

"I don't know. He's all right, I guess. He likes to give advice."

"Like what?"

"I don't know. All kinds of advice. One of his favorites is, 'If you'd stand up straight and smile once in a while you'd probably get a lot of attention from the girls.' "

"What does he know about it? Is he all stood up straight and smiling? Is that how he caught your mother's attention?"

"I don't know."

"I took your mother down to the lake, you know."

"I didn't know."

"I used to take her there. That's how she knows about it. She wouldn't even know about it if I hadn't taken her there." His father took a drink and handed the bottle across the seat. "Take some."

"That's all right."

"Go ahead, take some."

"I don't drink."

"You lie. When I was your age, I was putting 'em away. I mean putting. Like hell you don't drink."

"Not that."

"I was drinking whiskey at twelve years old," his father said. "Show me something."

Jim took the bottle from him and unscrewed the cap. It smelled sweeter than he thought it would, but he still didn't like the smell. He took a quick drink; the whiskey tingled his tongue and the roof of his mouth and then burned a trail down his throat. It made him shiver. He handed the bottle back to his father.

"Hang on to it, son. Give it another try or two. Come on, show me something."

It was an hour and a half drive to the lake. His father never directly said that it was their destination, but where else would he be going? His father looked straight ahead, keeping his eyes steadily on the road as it came into the yellow arc of the headlights. His father was thinking and every so often the right corner of his mouth would twitch and he'd make a small clicking noise. He watched his father; he did the same thing when he was thinking. He watched his father, looking for clues as to how else he might be like him. James. No one ever called him that; that was his father's name. He'd seen pictures of his father as a child; everybody always commented on how much they resembled each other at the same age. He guessed it was true, but they didn't look alike now. There were a couple of features, he noticed. He had his father's eyebrows—not bushy like his, but thick and dark, darker than their hair. He had the same shape ears, although his father's earlobes were attached. He was glad that his own weren't; the way they looked on his father kind of creeped him out. His father noticed him looking at him.

"You want to drive?"

"I can't."

"Another year. I should have you drive now. You want to drive?"

"I'd better not."

"Have it your way, Alice," his father said and turned his gaze back to the road.

Surfeit. His father turned off the main road and they made their way down a soggy dirt road for a mile or two. He pulled the car onto the shoulder and turned off the lights and then the engine. It was completely black. There were no stars and no lights visible anywhere around them. His father fished around in the duffel bag with no success. He opened the door to activate the dome light and pulled out a small flashlight. He put the duffel bag over his shoulder and zipped it closed again. "Come on," his father said and stepped out of the car and into the night.

The ground was still muddy from the rain, but it was starting to freeze now that it was cold, forming a crunchy crust on top. He followed his father across the road and down a shallow slope and into a large group of trees. His father put his hand in front of the flashlight to diffuse the light, but only blocked all of the light. "Hand me your hat," he said and Jim gave him the stocking cap he had been wearing. His father put the cap over the beam of the light. "I don't want anyone to see us, before we see them," his father said. Jim could barely see anything in front of them.

They made their way through the trees until they saw the lights of the cabin. His father turned off the flashlight and they slowly and quietly made their way from the trees, across the open grass, and to the cabin. There was no car outside, but his father motioned him to stay put while he moved around the outside, looking through each window to see if anyone was inside.

"It's empty," his father said.

They both went and checked the door. It was locked. All of the windows were latched as well, except a small one in the bathroom at the back of the cabin, facing the woods. "Can you fit through there?" his father asked. Jim nodded. "When you get inside, come let me in the front door."

Jim climbed through the window and went to the front door. His father entered the cabin and locked and put the chain across the door. There was mud on the floor from the boy's boots. "Smear that around," his father said.

The cabin had a large living area with a fireplace and sofa and two wingback chairs, a bedroom, and a bathroom. His father walked around, checking the dresser drawers and the bathroom. "They didn't even unpack," he muttered and went to the closet. He pulled out two suitcases and handed one to Jim.

"Open that," he told his son.

Jim knew it was his mother's suitcase. He placed it on the bed and unzipped the case and flipped it open. His father had opened his duffel bag and began pulling out small sacks of flour, sugar, and salt. He had bottles of mustard and ketchup and honey. He had wrenches and pliers and screwdrivers.

"I don't know about this," Jim said.

"It's a prank, a harmless prank. It's funny." His father

examined the sweaters and jeans he found in the suitcase. "This guy's giving you advice?" He filled the front pockets of a pair of jeans with ketchup and folded them and put them back in the case.

"Let's get to it," he said and handed the flour and honey to Jim.

Jim hesitated. "Come on, show me something," his father said and went into the bathroom.

His father placed all the towels and washcloths in the bathtub, still neatly folded, and soaked them. He shut off the water to the toilet and the sink. He then moved to the bedroom, where his son was pouring salt and flour over the pillowcases and in between the sheets.

"Take a shit in their bed," his father said.

"That's disgusting."

"It's not disgusting. That's a legitimate prank. That's an Ivy League, Skull and Bones, fraternity type of prank that people think is hilarious."

"You do it then."

"Your mother would recognize my mess in a second. It would be a dead giveaway."

"It won't get done then."

"Half-assed. It's going to be half-assed," his father said and began working on disconnecting the television.

Jim put all of the clothes back into the cases and then duct-taped them shut. He smeared the duct tape with honey and poured sugar over them. His father returned to the bathroom and placed the wet towels carefully back on the racks so they wouldn't look disturbed. He removed the lightbulbs from the fixtures in the bathroom and then did the same in the living room. His father put the lightbulbs in a pillowcase and stomped on the case, smashing the glass. Then he sprinkled the shards on the hardwood floor in the living room area.

"Don't do that," Jim said.

"Already done."

Jim turned away from his father and started toward the bedroom when he felt the smack at the back of his head from his father's open right hand.

"You've got your mother's mouth," his father said, then laughed. "Come on, this is fun. Have fun."

"Let's get out of here," Jim said.

"One last thing," his father said.

They were both covering the extra pillows and blankets with mustard when they heard the doorknob turn and the door stop as it met the chain's resistance. Jim rushed into the bathroom and made his way out the window. He didn't even think about his father; he ran toward the darkness of the trees. He heard a window fly open behind him and heard glass breaking. He glanced over his shoulder and saw his father make his way out of a bedroom window and run through the shallow swath of light and into the darkness to his left. Jim entered the woods and veered to his left on a diagonal path, hoping to intersect with his father.

He ran for a few seconds and then stopped and listened for any sound his father might make. He could hear the lake, the water falling against and away from the shore. They'd come all this way and he wasn't even going to get to see the lake. Maybe he could convince his father to stay the night and they could come look at it in the morning.

He looked around in the darkness. He could still see the light from the cabin behind him, but there was nothing but blackness in front of him. He started running away from the light, the cold ground crunching underneath his feet, and then stopped again. He thought he saw a faint light moving in front of him. "Hey," he called out in a whisper. There was no answer. The light went out. He waited for a few seconds but it didn't return. He continued to make his way through the trees.

As he saw the end of the woods, he noticed the light again. He stopped. The light suddenly became brighter, the harsh beam swinging across his face and then going out. He waited for his eyes to adjust back to the darkness and then walked to where the light had come from. His father was leaning against a tree, catching his breath.

"The car's just up the road," his father said. "We'd better get the hell out of here."

They walked out of the trees and up the shallow slope and onto the road. They hadn't taken more than a few steps when the headlights of a car appeared. They could see their car parked in front of the lights. They both stopped and the red-and-blue lights began spinning on top of the vehicle behind their car. An officer approached them, shining a flashlight in their faces, and said, "Put the bag down." His father dropped the duffel bag on the road and the officer led them back to the police car.

Intimation. Jim didn't know what had happened to his father. They had separated them once they entered the station. The arresting officer, Falco, took Jim into the captain's office and sat him down in a chair in front of the cluttered desk. It wasn't much of an office, especially for a captain. The name on the desk was LaBruno. The Bruno. He wondered if the captain looked like his name sounded. Jim LaBruno. That wasn't bad. It had to suck to be a cop's kid, though. Jim LaBruno still wasn't bad; it was better than what he had. A dictionary rested on top of a pile of papers. He could tell by the faded red cover and the embossed gold letters. If he had his list with him he could get his homework done while he waited around.

"You want anything to drink?" Falco asked him. He shook his head. Officer Falco sat down in the chair next to him.

"You ever been arrested before?"

"No."

"You ever been in trouble before? With the police?"

"Never."

"How about your father?"

"Not that I know of."

"That's right. No priors. So why'd you do this then?"

"We were just pulling a prank, I guess."

"The minute you entered the cabin, it was a lot more than a prank. And then there's the damage."

"It was just harmless stuff we did."

"The door was broken to reenter the cabin, and a window was broken on your way out. That's property damages that have to be addressed and restitution made."

"That wasn't our intent," Jim said. Mr. Gaines would have liked the use of *intent*. It was one of those words he always liked, with different meanings, depending on how it's used. He couldn't remember if it had been on a list before or not.

"Whose idea was it anyway?" Officer Falco asked.

"I don't know. Mine, I guess."

"Have you been drinking alcohol?"

He shook his head.

"How about your father? Has he been drinking?"

"A little, maybe."

The officer laughed. "A lot, maybe. Your parents aren't divorced?"

"Separated."

"How long?"

"About eight months, I guess."

"And how long has she been dating someone else?"

"A couple of months."

"Do you like this guy your mother's dating?"

"He's all right."

"Do you have anything you want to say to the both of them?"

"Not really."

"Well, you'd better think of something, because they're going to come down and get you in a while. We just have to process some paperwork and then you can go."

Venial. His mother and the boyfriend were standing in the small lobby; she went outside as soon as she saw him. He started to walk toward the door but the boyfriend stopped him.

"She's pretty upset."

He stopped and they both stood in the lobby. When she didn't return, the boyfriend went outside and he followed. His mother was sitting in the passenger seat and he went around the back of the car and sat behind the driver's seat. They all sat for a minute without talking. The only sound in the car was the hot air rushing out of the vents. The boyfriend kept looking over at the passenger seat and then got back out of the car and went back inside. Jim's mother finally turned around and looked at him.

"Despite your best efforts, you're not going to ruin my weekend," she said. It sounded rehearsed, which Jim thought indicated that she really meant it. "Don't think this is the end of it. It's just the beginning. We'll deal with you on Sunday." She turned away from him and stared down at her feet, maybe at the glove compartment.

His father came out with the boyfriend and they both got in the car. "Happy Valentine's Day, sweetheart," his father said. His wife didn't look at him, didn't even acknowledge that she had heard anything. "Thanks just the same. I mean that. Where'd you guys go eat? Martins? I bet it was Martins."

"Joke around all you want," she finally said. "You're in serious trouble. And you've got him in serious trouble too."

"It's not that serious. I'll explain everything when we come to court on Monday. I'll take care of it. It'll be all right."

They drove back to his father's car. Jim opened the door to get out but stopped when his father spoke.

"I'll send you a check for the bail, if that's all right."

"Okay," the boyfriend said.

Jim's father continued to sit in the backseat, smiling as he watched the couple in the front seat, until his mother finally said, "Get out." They stood and watched them drive off.

His father laughed. "She is pissed off. Man, is she pissed."

Jim didn't laugh. "What's going to happen on Monday?"

"We get to come back and see the judge."

"Then what?"

"We'll find out on Monday. Come on, let's go home."

His father started the car and then turned to his son. "Do you want to drive?"

"No."

His father put his left hand on the door latch. The dome light came on, illuminating the inside of the car. His father was smiling, a smile he had seen on himself before. "Come on," the older man said. "Show me something."

Highlands, NC

TABITHA SOREN

Paper Words

Sharon G. Flake

Okay. Now here's the truth. I ain't never been good at writing nothing. Till I got knocked up, and daddy locked me in my room for six months straight.

People think I'm lying when I tell 'em that. But it's true. Daddy was listening on the phone when I told my Boo I was pregnant. Before I could hang up, or run out the house with my Pooh Bear slippers on, Daddy drug me up the steps by my sore arm. Threw me on the bed like I was junk he found on the street when he hauling trash. And said for me not to go nowhere, less I wanted to end up dead or something.

It's just him and me here. Momma died giving birth to me. My brothers and sisters all grown and gone. I'm the one stuck with this old-ass man. He sixty-five. I'm fifteen. Now, do that make any sense?

When your father think you killed your momma, ain't no way he can like you. So it was easy, I guess, for him to lock me up here. He said it was gonna teach me a lesson. But he wanted to do it all along, I think. Lock me up. Hide everybody and everything from me; even the sun.

I thought he was kidding, at first. I mean, nobody would lock up a child, would they? Nail up the windows so the only fresh air you get is when you sniff it like glue, from the crack in the corner by the floor.

"Daddy," I said, the end of the first week. "I'll get rid of it, if you want."

He slipped a piece of paper under the door. The words were tall and strong, just like him. "Shut your mouth, till I tell you to talk," he said from the other side of the door. That was six months back. Before I learnt that my fingers could speak just as good as my throat.

The first words I wrote was this: "I hate you." I wrote 'em with a fat, green crayon. Smeared a booger on the backside of the paper. Slipped it under the door. When he picked it up, he got just what he deserved.

"Damn it!" he said, crumpling up the paper. Unlocking the door, and handing me my supper anyhow. "If you don't want no pee in your tea, you best not do that to me no more."

I didn't drink the ice tea. Or eat the sandwich and Jell-O. The baby was hungry. I sang her a song I made up. Never opened my mouth, though.

We live in the country. Got a hundred trees around us, but no houses. So ain't no neighbors dropping by for sugar. Or peeking out their windows into our house. Nobody to

ask Daddy how come they ain't seen me lately. School ain't
no different. I go when I feel like it. So even if the teacher
calls, all Daddy gotta say is, "She took off. Like she done
two years back. I'll call when I see her."

The first whole letter I wrote was to my boyfriend.

> Dear Bobby:
>   How come you ain't been by to see me? Don't you
> care 'bout your own child?
>   You ain't dating nobody else is you? 'Cause you
> know I love you.
>
>   Melody

Daddy gave me a stamp and a envelope. Said anybody I
wanted to write to, I could. "I ain't gonna stop you from
writing to nobody, gal. Shoot. Maybe they come take you
off my hands or something."

I ain't write my brothers and sisters, though. 'Cause
they think I lie 'bout everything anyway. So every day for a
month I just sat here. Not doing nothing but waiting for
my food. Reading the same magazine over and over again.
I ain't think about writing nothing like a poem, or a story,
till I seen a contest in the magazine. A person could win a
hundred dollars if their stuff got picked.

"What ya need money for if you ain't going nowhere,
ever?" I said to myself. But it was like my baby started talking to me. Saying she ain't gonna be inside me always. "Just
like you ain't gonna be stuck here for good." So I wrote
Daddy a note asking him for more paper. Pretty paper,
with flowers on it.

I figured he'd say no. But two days later, he unlocked the door. Handed me a box shaped like a peach. I opened it. Sniffed.

"Smell like they picked peaches this morning, and stomped 'em into the paper," Daddy said, handing me a ink pen.

I used up the whole box. Only got one good poem out it too.

> There's something deep inside of me,
> I have two eyes and still can't see,
> but I know if I'll leave it be,
> one day she might just rescue me.

Daddy ain't get mad at me for using all the paper up. And he mailed the poem. Two months later, a letter came for me. The first one I ever got. Daddy slipped it under the door. "What it say?" he asked.

I ain't know what to do. Figured maybe he was tricking me. Trying to see if I would speak up when I knew better.

"Gal. You gonna tell me what they said or not?"

I looked at my belly; like my baby knew what I should do. She kicked. I picked up last week's newspaper. Ripped off the top piece. Wrote Daddy a note:

"First place. One hundred dollars. They publishing it come spring."

Daddy ain't say nothing. But two days later hands me another box of paper. Grapes. My favorite.

I rubbed my belly. "Daddy," I wrote on my new, blue paper. "Is it raining out? Did the trees bloom yet?"

Daddy's eyes went to the window with the boards over top 'em. "Ain't nothing changed," he said, closing the door. Leaving me behind, like always.

I think my baby is making me smarter. 'Cause I ain't never know I had so many words in my head till she come along. I'm six months along now. Ain't seen no doctor. Daddy say I don't need none.

"What ya think we done before we had money for doctors? We took care our own," he said.

Maybe he right. I ain't been sick since I been in this room. And every day he give me vitamins, green things, and fruit. Today, my Baby Girl give me something too. Another poem.

> Baby Girl
> with baby curls
> warm inside of me.
> Do u know,
> what I know,
> that love is always free.
> Will u be, just like me
> stuck inside a room?
> Or strong enough to kick the stuff
> blocking you from the moon.

Daddy read the poem. Looked at me and walked out the room. For the next three days he ain't say nothing. Not even good morning. He dropped off my food, and walked out the room. Come Thursday, he was talking again. But words still couldn't come out my mouth. "Only paper words," he said, "till I say when."

Two days 'fore Baby Girl come, Daddy handed me a letter. "It's yours," he said, sitting down on my bed. Looking tired. Old.

Po-etic Places was spelled in fancy, baby blue letters all the way 'cross the top. The letter was to me. So was the check—five hundred dollars.

Daddy sent my poem in. Read about the contest at the post office. "Figured it wouldn't do no harm," he said, kicking mud off his boots.

"Daddy," I write. "Baby Girl is coming soon. A mother's gotta talk to her child—say her name. Sing her a made-up song. Walk her in the sun."

Daddy got up. Went to the covered window. I figured he was gonna finally set me free, so words came out my mouth before they shoulda. "Thank you, Daddy."

He stopped in his tracks. Stood with his back to me for fifteen minutes. I covered my face with my hand when he headed my way.

"One man," Daddy says, sitting down on my bed, "takes a box and makes a coffin. Another man takes a box and builds a shed. What you building, gal?"

Baby Girl kicks me right between the ribs. It's a sign, I know. But I don't know the right thing to say. Tears roll down my face. Words come to my lips thick and sweet as homemade chocolate. "Daddy," I say, clearing my throat, "I ain't building nothing special. Just trying to get myself out this here room."

I shut my eyes soon as I turn the words loose. I tell Baby Girl not to worry if she gets kicked or punched. "It don't never hurt for too long," I say. Only Daddy's fists never do come after us. And he don't shut the door behind him, when his flat feet take him out of the room.

I look out into the hall. But don't leave the room for two whole hours. "Go," I hear Baby Girl say. I wait till the front door shuts, and Daddy's truck takes off. "Go," she says, while I'm sliding my bare feet down the hall. Over the dusty stairs. Onto the front porch.

Baby Girl jumps. Kicks. Pushes hard against me when I walk out into the sun. I close my eyes. Sing Baby Girl a sweet song right there in my head. Let my fingers play in the light.

Excerpt from *Geography of Girlhood*

Three Poems About Bobby

Kirsten Smith

Motorbike

I follow the smell of motorbike home
because that's where my sister must be.
My sister has spent summer with her arms
wrapped around Bobby's waist,
racing through alleys and other parts unknown.
My sister is spangly with friends and people that
    love her.
My sister is a walking tiara.
She is everyone's prize
and the only thing she wants
is the smell of gasoline in her hair
and the taste of something
that doesn't taste like anything else
on her lips.

Behind My Sister's Back

Let's do something bad. I want to,
Bobby said, opening our fourth bottle,
popping the lid off the night.
He'd been thrown out of the junior prom
just after asking you to go steady
for the umpteenth time.
Five minutes later, you and I got in a fight
in the girls' bathroom because I was wearing
your favorite shirt.
So when Bobby offered me a ride, I took it.
We drove Route 1 with the windows down
and Bobby said that this was the road
he felt most reckless on,
as we scudded through the night,
through the foliage that hung low and close,
trees and shrubs that said come into me.
Some nights, he said, he wanted to just
drive off that road,
the reckless impulse was so strong
even you weren't enough to distract him.
We drove down to the marina
and we drank and drank
and before I puked into the sea,
we kissed, the boats
heaving and squeaking around us.
Later, on other nights, we did other bad things,
we hurt you because we could,
we spent nights behind your back,

waiting for you to notice
as we dog-paddled our way into danger,
thinking we were trouble waiting to happen,
high beams heading off into the magnetic dark.

Touching Bobby

You are the boyfriend of my sister,
a girl I'm not even sure I care about,
let alone love.
I am the girl who was always in her room,
sweating at the thought of your police record.
Now, when I see you waiting for me outside of
    school,
I am a bungle of hubcaps on a hot day,
desperate for someone to drive me off the lot.

You open the car door for me
and I want some of your bad boy
to rub off on my hands like newsprint.
I want to peer inside your mouth,
find out how the lies started and where.
As your blue-jeaned leg whispers against mine,
the smell of grade school,
of paste and geography texts,
rises around us, like the smell of something
already long gone,
like some powder
dropped on the ordinary world.

Breaking and Entering

David Levithan

People never change the place they hide their keys.

It was right after midnight. Back when it was summer, back when I had some reason to hope. Cody's parents were out of town for the weekend and Cody's keys were locked in his car, seven blocks away. He took me around back and we walked quietly through the night foliage, listening like thieves for the neighbors who would notice, the ones who might tell. I wasn't supposed to be there, wasn't supposed to be the boy Cody loved, wasn't supposed to notice when he moved the flowerpot and revealed the spare key underneath. He didn't say anything, didn't swear me to secrecy. He just held his breath a little as he squeezed past me to the door, ran inside so the alarm wouldn't sound. When I walked in, I had to call out for him. He reached me before I got to the light switch. We found ourselves in the dark.

Now it's afternoon, four months later. Cody is gone, but the key is still in its hiding place. I don't know what I'm doing here, only that I have to be here, doing this. Breaking and entering. The breaking has already happened, is always happening. So I reach for the key. I fit it into the lock. And I enter.

I should be in school. I should be enjoying the first breaths of the last gasp of my senior year. I should be living my days like they are the best days.

Cody is in a place I've never been, with people I've never met. Somehow I allowed him to step into the future without me.

From a schedule I saw back when all such things were hypothetical, I know he is sitting in an English class right now. I can picture him there. I can see him slumped back and doodling. I can see him after class, walking over the green. Or asleep in his dorm room, eyelids closed. The pattern of his breathing. I can see it clearly, and none of it is true. It is only my version, which is imagination.

This place is real. These steps are real. I am in his house, surrounded by the house silence that is not like breathing at all. There is only background. It is a sound like loneliness—enough to let you know you're there, but not enough to fill you with life.

I have very few memories of the kitchen, but it's still hard to be in here. It's wrong and it's stupid and it's hard. I can't deny what I'm doing anymore, not with the faucet dripping and cereal bowls in the sink. I remember the silver of the kitchen I saw that night when the refrigerator light knifed it open to us. Four in the morning, he could stand there naked and not be afraid. I wore his robe and took comfort in the thought that I was making it a little bit mine. Everything we did that night seemed so brave and so doomed. Brave because we felt doomed, doomed because we felt we'd always need to be brave. Even getting orange juice at four in the morning. Looking into that light.

I want him to know I'm here now.

I want him to know I'm here.

The sink drips and drips and drips. Cars pass outside. The key is still in my hand, fitting.

There are things he told me. His fear of stormy nights. The time he kissed a boy in summer camp, pretending it was a game. His father's affair. The strength of his love, even if he didn't always call it love.

I remember these things. They are my proof that we actually happened. He wouldn't have told me these things if I hadn't meant something to him. If he didn't find some meaning in me.

I drive past all the time. On my way to school. If I wanted to avoid it, I would have to choose to avoid it. Whether I passed or not, I'd be thinking about it. Where he once was, back when we were.

We'd said we'd keep in touch. But touch is not something you can do from a distance. Touch is not something you can keep; you can only remember a picture of touch. We should have said we'd keep in words. Because they are all we can string between us—words on a telephone line, words appearing on a screen. But they cause more complications than clarity. On the phone, there are always voices in his background. On the screen, there are always the sentences saying he has to go.

I know he is gone, but this house is not. That's the only way I can explain it. I cannot touch him, cannot press my hand against his body, cannot feel the warmth spread from his skin. The best I can do is touch the things he has touched the most. I just want a moment in his bed. To trace.

The stairway is lined with photographs. He is every year old. That night, he walked me through all the class pictures, all the bad haircuts and awkward smiles. The seven-year-old ring bearer and the fourteen-year-old on the lip of the Grand Canyon. He had a flashlight and he told the photographs like they were words in a long sentence. Then he turned the flashlight off. He took my hand and led me forward.

His room looks the same. His parents always leave the light on. To ward off burglars. To pretend someone is home. I don't have to touch the switch. I don't have to do anything but walk inside. I know he took things with him. I was there when the car left. I stood there camouflaged by his other friends in a group goodbye. I saw the milk crates of books and sheets and toiletries crammed into the back-seat and the twine-tied trunk. But the room doesn't seem to have suffered from the subtraction. Most of the books remain on the shelves; I see a copy of *Demian* and wonder if it's the one I gave him or the one he already had. I take some solace that there aren't two, that a book he would associate with me has made it to his room at college. I cling to the associations.

The bed is made, ready for his return. I put my face to the pillowcase, hoping it might smell like his echo. But instead it smells like laundry. I take off my shoes. I curl up on top of the sheets. I clutch.

We fought over who it would be easier for. He said I was lucky to be in the same place, to have such a familiar world around me, to have the friends here and the knowledge of where I was. I said he was lucky to be getting a new beginning, to be moving on.

I don't know what I thought I'd find by breaking in here. An envelope with my name on it, awaiting my arrival? Cody himself, standing in front of the closet, deciding what to wear? An entirely empty room, as robbed of his presence as I am? No, not really. Maybe all I wanted was what I find now: rest. Simple, uncomplicated rest.

The light fades. The day ends. The door opens and I don't hear, because I'm asleep. It isn't until she's in the room that I stir. I sense her presence before I can register it. She stands there for a beat before saying anything.

"Peter?"

I open my eyes. There is light, there is color, and there is Mrs. Baxter standing in the doorway, looking like she's come home to find all the furniture rearranged.

I am surprised she knows my name. I've met her probably a dozen times, but it was always in passing. I was a sound in another room, a door about to close, a phone call answered before she got to it. I'd never felt like a boy with a name to her. Cody had wanted to keep me separate.

"Hi, Mrs. Baxter," I say, sitting up and turning out of bed. Staring at my shoes unlaced on the floor.

"Is Cody here?" she asks. But she's looked around. She knows the answer.

"I don't think so," I tell her. If I bend over to put on my shoes, I will have to turn my head entirely away from her. And that seems rude, so I just sit there.

I always thought Cody looked more like his father—the same shoulders, the same dark hair. But there's something in Mrs. Baxter's eyes that looks familiar. I don't know whether it's their shape or color or just the way she is looking at me now, trying to piece the situation into sense. I get that glint of Cody from her.

"How did you get in?" This is said calmly, almost kindly. She's not alarmed. I don't get that from her.

"I used the key." I've let go of it, lost it in the folds of the blanket. I reach over for it now, hold it in my palm for a moment before offering it out, back to her.

She doesn't take it. She has her own keys in her hand. Unjangling car keys and house keys and probably office keys. Her hair is shorter than I remember. When Cody left, she must have cut her hair.

I reach for my shoes and then stop. I feel the key in my hand and I stop. I don't look right at her and I don't look all the way away from her. She is standing next to Cody's desk and I am looking at the photos on the bulletin board. I am looking for me. I am looking for some sign of me.

If we were strangers, she would be calling the police. If I had been a part of her life, if she had known me, we would be talking. But instead we're somewhere between strangers and familiar. So the questions fill the room in their silence.

He pulled away from her. He never told me that, maybe

didn't even know it. But all the times Cody talked about his father and everything his father did wrong, he never said anything about his mother. Not to me.

I know the situation is my fault, so maybe that's why I finally make the questions audible, why I finally say, "You're probably wondering why I'm here."

And she doesn't say anything. For just a moment, she gives me a look that makes me think that, yes, it's possible she *does* know exactly why I'm here, more than I know myself.

"I'm so sorry," I continue. And it's like the last word is a hurdle and I can't leap it, because something in the word snags my voice and suddenly I am giving everything up. I am letting my shoulders fall and I am feeling myself become the absence, feeling myself become that gasp and sob.

I could never say what I was to him. He never let me know, because maybe he was afraid if I did, then everyone would know.

But keeping my guard up has made me feel so unguarded. And now I just want it to end. I've always wanted the happy ending, but now I'll just settle for the ending.

Here. In his room. How had we managed to erase the rest of the world? Because that is what it took for us to crawl into the naked silence, into the truth of the thing, into the doomed and the brave.

Now the light is on and his mother is here and I am on the edge of his bed and my head is in my hands. My eyes are open and I'm not seeing a thing because I am so lost inside.

I hear the hit of the keys as she puts them down on the desk. I see her legs as she walks over. I feel the weight of her as she sits on the bed next to me, not touching.

"Peter?" she says gently.

And I say it again. "I'm sorry." And again.

He is so far away and he doesn't feel it like I do. He doesn't feel it.

We sit there. Breathing, thinking. There is the slight, amber smell of alcohol in the air. Her breathing.

"You don't have to be sorry," she says. "I'm just a little confused."

I can tell from the sound of her voice that she's not looking at me, just as I'm not looking at her. We're both looking in front of us now. At the empty doorway.

"You miss him," she says. And my first instinct is to deny it. Deny us. Deny her. Deny myself. To admit one thing is to admit everything. It has always been that way.

So instead I wonder what my silence says. Because even if I cannot say *yes,* cannot say *so much,* I also can't bring my voice to say *no,* to say *I don't really miss him at all.*

Quietly, so quietly, she says, "I know."

I turn to her then. And her eyes are closed. Her coat is still on. She looks like she is about to shiver. Then she opens her eyes, sees me, and smiles. Not a big smile, or even a welcoming one. But a small, rueful smile. A sad smile. A kindred smile.

"It's not easy," she says, in that voice that mothers have, that mix of unwanted knowledge and small consolation. "Whatever you had—I don't know exactly what it was, and that's fine. But it must not be easy for you. You miss him, and that's okay. But you have to figure that if it's too hard to hang on, then maybe you should let go."

I want to ask if he's mentioned me.

"What is his room like?" I ask instead. "Up there."

She looks at me for a moment, deciding something, then says, "It's fairly small. Not much bigger than this room, but for two people. His bedspread is blue. It matches the carpet, which is something we couldn't have known. We got him a refrigerator. One of the small ones. His roommate seemed very nice. I think they get along."

"Does he call?"

She nods. "Yes. We talk for a few minutes. Every few days."

If I had been the same age. If I had gone to the same school. If I was in that room right now. There's no way to know if we would have lasted. There's no way to be sure, and plenty of reasons to doubt it. I just wish I'd had the chance. That is one of the things I miss the most—the chance to make it work.

The whole time I thought that I was figuring him out, wearing down his hesitations. But really I was wearing myself down in order to spend that one last hour, that one last sentence.

"Peter," Mrs. Baxter says. And it's almost the way he says it. The ghost of his intonations. "You can't do this. Look at me." I do, and it's not his eyes I see. No, it's something completely separate. A different kind of concern. "Do you understand? You can't do this."

I start to say I'm sorry again. For using the key. For being here, when all she probably wanted to do tonight was take off her coat, sort through the mail, wait for the call.

"It doesn't work," she continues, staring ahead. "What you're feeling right now doesn't work. You can't wander around and think the wandering will call them back. Believe me. I know you don't want to hear the long view, but let me tell you. You are so young. I know it's none of my business. But still."

She sounds surprised by her own urgency, by the fact that she is talking to me this way. Like I am getting all the advice she never gets a chance to give.

She stands then. Puts her hand on my shoulder and lifts herself off the bed. Walks to the doorway, then turns back around.

"Say goodbye," she tells me. "Not to him, but to this part of it. You can stay as long as you want. But don't do this again. This is the last time."

I know that's not why I came here. But suddenly it feels like it is.

She picks her keys off of his desk and looks at me, at the room, one long time before she steps into the hall. I hear her bedroom door close behind her. Cody's door remains open.

I don't need any souvenirs. I'm sure there are things that I could take that he would never know were missing. But I already have an unlabeled collection of things that are ours. We would ink our skin blue and sign messages with our thumbprints. We bought our favorite movies for each other. We made our own yearbooks to sign for each other, a month or two before he left.

The yearbook I made him could be with him now, or maybe just hidden somewhere in this room. I say goodbye to knowing the answer. I say goodbye to the sheets that don't smell like him. I say goodbye to the robe that's forgotten what I felt like. I say goodbye to the part of myself that misses him so much. I say goodbye to hope, but I also say goodbye to hope's disappointment.

I turn the light off as I leave. Then I remember, and turn it back on. Leave the room as I found it, but not untouched.

I call out goodbye to his mother. She calls goodbye in return.

I head back down the stairs. I head through the kitchen. I open the back door, then close it behind me. It is only then that I realize I still have the key. I go to the flowerpot, which I hadn't moved back in place. It is dark now outside but I can still see the outline of where the pot should be sitting, the faint impression left by the key. I return the key to its hiding place, then conceal it once more.

People say goodbye, and then they take one last look. I am a few steps away when I turn to his window. And there, as I watch, the light goes out. The door closes, and I walk away.

Eyepoker

MO WILLEMS

Concept

Benjamin M. Foster

We'd all been sent to Concept—the famous, so-called therapeutic community—for the same reason. Oh, the particulars were different—there were junkies and drunks and whores and rich kids who had tried to kill themselves, even a guy whose father had sent him here for being gay—and there were a lot of people like me: fucked-up teenage kids who cut school and smoked a lot of pot. But those were the particulars. The real reason we were sent here was because somebody somewhere decided that we weren't fit to live in society. You can send an adult to prison, but what do you do with a teenager who's out of control? In those days, you sent him to a mental hospital, or waited until he got arrested and thrown in a detention center. And when none of

Some of the names in this piece have been changed.

that worked, you sent him to Concept, because he was clearly not going to learn from his mistakes. If you were in Concept, you were out of control.

So how did they control us? They let us run the show.

There were forty people in our house. There were three staff members during the day and one at night. During the day we worked. Each resident had a job in a different department—the Kitchen, the Business Office, the Service Crew, or any of the others. We went to school in the evenings in the trailers behind the house. When we weren't in school, sleeping, eating, or working, we were in encounter groups, screaming our lungs out at each other.

New residents started at the bottom and worked their way up. If you followed the rules and didn't talk shit about other people, or talk about what you'd done or were planning to do on the outside, you moved up. If you screwed up, you got a "haircut"—a screaming session delivered by three or four of your peers—or a "general meeting," where you'd be stood up in front of everyone in your house so they could scream at you, and so the house director could run you down. And you got "shot down," which meant you lost your job and were forced to clean toilets, wash dishes, or scrub out garbage cans while wearing shorts and shoes with no laces. The only equalizer was encounter groups, where you could scream and swear at anybody else in the group, regardless of their rank.

By the time I'd been there almost a year, I'd received over a hundred and fifty haircuts and ten general meetings, I'd been shot down over twenty times, and I'd been in the corner seven times. The corner was where you were put when you were out of control. You'd sit in the corner of a room, usually in the older trailer known as the old schoolhouse, with a P.O.—personal observer—watching you to make sure you didn't split or destroy anything or try to kill yourself.

The staff stayed in the background most of the time. They ran the groups and the general meetings, and they approved the punishments that were handed out after haircuts, like the signs and costumes. If you talked back to one of your superiors, you might get a haircut and a sign reading, "Ask Me Why I Can't Hold My Mud." If you laughed in a haircut, you'd get a clown mouth painted around your lips. If a girl came on to a guy, she'd get a hooker costume. She'd be dressed up like a 1930s harlot and she'd have to carry around a sign reading "42nd Street." If you whined or acted like a little kid, you'd get a baby costume—a sheet wrapped around your groin like a diaper, and a bonnet and rattle to go with it. If you then really walked the line, you'd be able to take off the sign or costume in a week.

You'd think that we all could've collectively rebelled, but we never did and as far as we knew, nothing like that had ever happened in Concept. Most of us who had been there for a while didn't want to delay our return to the real world by taking part in an uprising. We did our jobs. When we saw somebody break a rule we "booked an incident" on them, which meant ratting each other out to the shingle expeditor, who wrote down all infractions in a notebook to be dealt with later in a haircut. We took part in groups and we did well in school. We'd learned the hard way that rebelling got you nowhere.

There were seven coordinators, one for each of the departments. I was the coordinator of the Kitchen, which was one of the highest positions in the house. I'd been up and down, and up was a lot better. I'd spent countless hours hunched over the large sink at the back of the kitchen—what we called the "back pan"—with a Brillo pad, trying to wash pans coated with layers of scrambled egg or pots caked with burnt tomato sauce. I'd scrubbed and mopped the kitchen floors, and cleaned the grill and the hoods above the stove. I'd washed the walls and scrubbed out the garbage cans. But now I was running the crew, and I assigned those jobs. I prepared and delivered the meals for the staff meetings. I made sure the night crews—the ones who stayed up all night doing head counts in dorms—had their meals prepared. I did the weekly evaluations of my crew, and I reported to staff whether I thought the shot-downs deserved a cigarette break or not. And when my morning work shift was interrupted for a general meeting, I put on a fresh pot of coffee, because when our director, Al Kesselman, gave a G.M., he went through about a pack and a half of butts and a gallon of coffee.

I was issuing a pull-up—an order spoken as a firm suggestion—to one of my workers to clean up some of the dirt he'd missed with the dustpan when Mike DeJong, the coordinator on duty, came into the kitchen to let me know we'd be starting a G.M. soon. He motioned me over to the sink.

G.M.s were supposed to be a surprise to everyone but the coordinators.

"We're just waiting on Carr," he said quietly.

Sean Carr had been a coordinator up until two weeks ago when he'd been shot down for stealing food from the kitchen. He'd come in only two weeks before me, just a little over eleven months ago. He was working his way back up to coordinator but at the moment he worked for me as a department head, a midlevel position that didn't call for a lot of manual labor.

"I was just going to talk to him," I answered.

"I've got a few more haircuts to knock out first," he said. "Can you just let Al know?"

"Yeah."

I told my crew to take a break and we headed out the back door to sit on the steps and smoke. Smoking wasn't allowed during G.M.s, and you never knew how long they were going to last. Carr asked me if I was growing a mustache.

"Yeah," I said, rubbing the wispy strands on my upper lip with my thumb and forefinger. "Perk of the gig."

"I know," he answered.

I started walking over to the Dumpster and motioned for him to follow me. I pretended like I was pointing something out in the Dumpster, like I was asking him to clean it, or more likely, assign a shot-down to the job.

"Jake's getting G.M.'d today," I said, keeping my voice low.

"For what?"

"He threw a chair at the window in the old schoolhouse last night." Jake Rossen was in the corner and had been for three weeks.

Sean didn't say anything. Throwing a chair wasn't that big a deal, not if you were in the corner.

"Thing is," I continued, "Al wants to break him. He didn't *say* so, but he wants to break him. We had a coordinators' meeting this morning and Al was blaming *us,* saying that we're running a loose house."

"That sucks."

"It sucks for *you* if we get shot down or demoted."

"What do you mean?" He was playing dumb.

"I mean that I've been letting you get away with murder and we both know it, and if I lose my job, you're fucked."

He took a drag off his Newport and exhaled slowly.

"So what's up?" he asked.

"Jake stole a pair of your jeans last week."

"Yeah. Stole Sontay's Rolex, too. Got 'em back, though."

"Look, you know what I'm supposed to do. I'm supposed to tell you that you'll be helping out the house. You'll be setting a good example. But you know it's bullshit. The prick stole your jeans and laughed in your face about it. The coordinators want you to go in the ring."

"Against Jake."

"Yeah."

"I can take him." He said it more as a question than a statement. He and Jake were the same size—all three of us were, actually, only Sean and Jake had muscle; I looked like I had limp strands of spaghetti hanging from my shirt-sleeves. Sean Carr had been a drunk before Concept but he'd also been a football star, and he wrestled and played basketball and baseball as well. He'd only started smoking in Concept, and only because not smoking wasn't really an option; a few weeks engulfed in the clouds of ubiquitous cigarette smoke in the house and you were as good as addicted anyway. But in spite of his pack-a-day habit and the relatively sedentary lives we lived, Sean did his best to stay in shape by doing a few sets of push-ups and sit-ups each morning. We were in the same dorm and he'd been trying to get me to work out with him, but I preferred the comfort of bed to sweating and grunting on the floor every morning at seven thirty.

"He's pretty tough," I answered. "But yeah, you'll take him." Jake *was* tough—I'd seen him in the ring as the good guy once, fighting at Al's request against some new resident who had taken a swing at his department head. He'd demolished the kid. But Sean matched up well with him, and I figured he'd beat Jake because he'd have the crowd on his side. Besides that, Sean would want to win more. He had a reason to be pissed off at Jake and he'd never liked him anyway; I always thought Sean kind of looked down on the rest of us because it was easy to tell that we'd been fuck-ups before Concept. Sean had been a fuck-up too, but he'd had a veneer of respectability because he'd been a jock. It just wouldn't sit right with him to be beaten by one of us.

The other reason I figured Sean would win was simply that I wanted him to. I hated Jake Rossen. He had a face like a rat and a personality to go with it. Jake never booked anybody for anything unless he was getting revenge. He was the worst kind of hypocrite; he got on guys for breaking the prison code of never ratting but he'd break it himself as soon as it served his purposes. He was always stealing stuff from guys—watches, clothes, cassettes—and he always acted like you were the jerk for being pissed about getting ripped off by him. Whoever was in on his latest harebrained scheme to split was his friend and whoever steered clear of him was his enemy. He had a way of making you feel like a dick for being true to yourself, especially if you weren't willing to look the other way when he stole from somebody or tried to get you to split with him. There were really only two ways to get out of Concept: play the game by the rules, or split and hope you didn't get caught. Almost everybody got caught, so almost everybody ended up cooling down and playing by the rules. But Jake made you feel like a chump for doing it. Doing things his way was idiotic, if not suicidal, but you still ended up feeling like a jack-off after he had sneered and laughed at you, so you couldn't simply take the attitude that what he did was his own business; you just couldn't help hating the guy. I wanted to see him get his ass kicked, if only to see that annoying smirk wiped off his face for a few minutes.

Sean said he'd go in the ring and I told him I'd come and get him when it was time. I stubbed out my cigarette on the asphalt and tore the filter into little pieces—field-stripping, we called it.

"Let's go," I yelled. Everybody went back to work.

I told Sean to keep an eye on the crew and left the kitchen, walking through the dining room, the hallway where the Service Crew closet was, through the Business Office, and up the main hall past the coordinator's office to the living room. I knocked on the door.

"Come in." It was Al. Al was always in the living room when the coordinator's office was being used for haircuts—there was no dedicated office for the staff. He was sitting on the couch in front of the TV, flipping through the papers on his clipboard.

I walked inside, closing the door behind me, and stood next to the couch.

"I talked to Sean," I said. "He'll do it."

Al was very good at keeping a poker face. Even when he got angry, you got the feeling it was deliberate and measured, though such observations were usually made sometime after he'd managed to jelly your legs and send your heart on a cardiac adventure with a blistering haircut or a harrowing G.M. He was a big man—over six feet tall—and built like a human bulldozer. It was never clear which parts of him were muscle or fat; he was just *big*, like a 270-pound cinder block. He kept his hair cut short, but even after a trim the back of his neck was a mass of angry black specks that stubbornly refused to be sheared off by any barber's clippers. His beefy face was mostly hidden behind a neatly clipped black beard that, in spite of conscientious grooming, seemed to start just under his eyes and become one with his chest hair. His meaty paws appeared to be capable of crushing your windpipe in a millisecond or two, and the look in his eyes often suggested he was considering just that. When he got pissed off, his face turned all sorts of crazy shades of red and purple and although you knew he'd never touch you, you always kind of feared for your life.

But behind his physical appearance and frightening demeanor was a man of complexity and intelligence; he could quote Voltaire at length and he seemed to have most of the works of Emerson committed to memory. But for Al, a big part—maybe the only part—of caring meant being tough; he understood that people like us took a mile for every inch we were given, and he refused to baby anyone. Nor did he aspire to be a father figure to anyone; Al was our *director* and so he directed us from an emotional distance, preferring for us to find support from each other as he kept himself on the perimeter of our lives. Al was a scary-looking guy, but he would have been just as intimidating if he'd been five foot two with a lisp.

Al was a Concept graduate from the early seventies. He had been offered a staff position at Concept upon graduation and he'd never left. Al had been on staff for thirteen years and running the house for twelve. Just under fifteen years ago, he'd been robbing houses and businesses in Boston for heroin money. Now he was in charge of the lives of everybody who walked through the front door. He knew every angle, every line of bullshit, every ridiculous lie that we could think up. He'd seen it all a thousand times. And he knew better than to let any of us know what he was thinking. But this morning, he looked relieved. It was a brief look, and when he saw me looking at him, the relief left his face as quickly as it had crept in.

"He's still piss— He's still mad about Jake stealing his jeans last week."

Al stroked his beard.

"We can't make this about a personal grudge," he said.

I really hated Al. In Concept we spent most of our lives attacking each other for playing games, for not saying what we meant, for being manipulative, all to please the staff and get a job promotion, get one step closer to freedom. And Al was very good at keeping everything on the up-and-up. In fact, I'll even go so far as to say that he really wanted to help us. I truly believe he did. But think about it. You go from being a deadbeat, useless junkie—no education, no job skills, no future—to being a well-paid employee of a so-called therapeutic community. Wouldn't you worry about your job? You're working for Concept, known worldwide for turning lost causes into model citizens. Parents, school systems, and state agencies all over the country—all over the world—send you their kids. They don't know what you do and they don't care. All they know and care about is that you get results. So you'd damn well better get results. And Jake Rossen was not cooperating.

I hated Al, not because he was *wrong* but because everything became a battle of wills in the end, and Al was always there pulling the strings. He had a massively unfair advantage, which might not have been a big deal if I'd been sure his motives were pure. But nobody's motives are ever completely pure.

The main part of my job as coordinator was to make sure that everybody underneath me toed the line. We knew how to tear somebody down and build him back up the *right* way. Maybe that's not a trick at all, maybe it should be called something that doesn't sound so cheap—like a method. After all, it did help people. It even helped me, at least some. But knowing how to play the game and how to make other people play the game was how we kept our jobs, and it was about the only way to get out of there in under twenty-four months. And as much as I hated Al, I respected him. He wasn't a phony. And like I said, I really believe that he cared; he really believed the *methods* that were used in Concept were saving lives. But even though Al treated us coordinators like equals, at the end of the day he went home to his wife. We went to sleep in a bunk underneath some juvenile delinquent from New Hampshire or Chicago or California. So we *weren't* his equals, and I felt if I ever let myself believe that, I'd really be a sucker. So I resented him for trying to treat me like an equal. Normal people could manage to take what they could get from the situation—enjoy the perks and not get too upset over the hypocrisy of acting like we weren't always subject to the whims of the staff and even the other residents—but I guess I wasn't very normal, because I had to think the thing to death. That's why I never lasted very long as a coordinator.

So I let his statement hang there in the air for a minute before I said anything. And it sat there like an elevator fart and I looked him right in the eye, not saying anything. I held his stare for as long as I could, trying to look innocent, but not too much. I wanted him to know that I knew what was going on. Finally, I looked away and said, "A grudge isn't the main thing. The main thing is, Sean wants to work his way back up to coordinator. He wants to do the right thing—set an example. He knows in his heart that he's a coordinator. He's just trying to act like one."

"Good, good." This was comfortable ground for Al. "Carr will have his gig back in no time." He paused and looked down for a minute. Which was funny, because Al never looked down. He looked you in the eye, and you always turned away first.

"What's this about the jeans?" he asked.

"It's nothing," I said. "I was just saying, it's not like Jake's his *friend* or anything."

"Well," he answered, looking up to meet my eyes again, "you're never going to get along with everybody you live with."

"That's right."

"That's what we have groups for."

"Absolutely."

He stubbed out his cigarette in the ashtray to his right.

"What's for lunch?" he asked.

"Cold subs," I answered. "They'll keep."

"Call a G.M."

I told the ramrod of broadcasting to call everyone to the dining room and then I hurried back to the kitchen. Carr was slicing cold cuts when the announcement came over the P.A.

I told my crew to drop what they were doing and go to the dining room. They left and I put on a fresh pot of coffee.

Within two minutes, the residents in the dining room had stacked the tables at the back of the room and set up the chairs in rows, leaving an aisle down the middle. There was a stage at the back of the room; I'd always thought that running a G.M. with the guilty party standing on the stage would be more dramatic, but Al knew better. Drama was important, but the guy getting the G.M. had to be on the same level as the other residents for the rush.

I sat on the aisle in the front row, right next to the coffee bar. Some of the residents were talking, and I gave them a couple of minutes before I stood up and told them to quiet down. Carr walked over and sat down next to me. Matthew Kurz walked in next. Matthew was outside staff—among the first wave that Concept had. Prior to Matthew, all staff had been graduates of the program. Matthew was a college graduate who specialized in adolescent psychology and he was our assistant director. He was being groomed for a director gig for a new house that was being built down the hill near the lake.

You could hate Al and still respect him. Matthew would never have my respect, and not only because he hadn't been one of us; I believed that Matthew had been picked on and beaten up by people like us, and he'd never forgotten it. His spotty beard barely covered a face riddled with acne scars. He was a sadist. He demanded subservience, and he got it, because when he was crossed, he was cruel. He was barely able to contain his glee when he shot a kid down, or ordered a sign to be placed around a kid's neck, and when somebody in the corner had to be put into restraints when Matthew was on duty, the kid's personal observer always had to call him to come back and remove them within a half hour because the kid's hands would start turning blue.

Matthew poured himself a cup of coffee, taking his time adding the cream and sugar, and then he leaned over to me and Sean.

"Ready for the show?"

"I'm ready," answered Sean.

"Yeah," I said, giving him one of those nods of camaraderie and hating myself for doing it. Matthew took up his customary post next to the coffee bar. Staff always stood during a G.M., no matter how long it lasted.

Mike DeJong strutted in carrying his clipboard. Al strode in behind him. He had a peculiar gait, like a man who was hurrying to make an appointment but didn't want to break out into a run. Al poured a cup of coffee and headed to the left side of the front of the room, near the window, which was where he always started G.M.s. He took a sip of coffee and then put the cup down on the window ledge and leaned against it, half-sitting. He pulled a pack of Merits from the pocket of the shirt underneath his sweater and shook a cigarette loose.

"Where's my chief?" he asked, addressing the crowd. The chief was the head of security for the house.

Evelyn Hart stood up and said, "Here."

"Is everyone here?"

She looked down to her left, where one of her expeditors was fumbling with a paper on his clipboard. He finally got it loose and handed it to her. She scanned it quickly and said, "Everybody's here except for the corner people and their P.O.s."

Al lit his cigarette and exhaled.

"Let's get started."

The room tensed as it always did just before a G.M. started. The strain was worse on the people in lower positions because they knew they might be called to the front of the room; the only time they relaxed was when someone else was standing in the front of the room. G.M.s could focus on one individual, or five, or all of us. Those of us in higher positions breathed easier after the first person was called up, unless we were pretty sure we were going to be singled out. When strength was G.M.'d by surprise, it was usually as a group—all department heads or coordinators—and we were almost always dealt with first. But even though the coordinators had just had a meeting with Al and Matthew about the G.M., we knew we could always be called up before Rossen. I scanned my memory like I did before every G.M. What had I done wrong lately? Nothing? Okay, who had I pissed off? Was there a lot of trouble in the house lately? That was a bad sign—if things started getting a little out of control, the coordinators were blamed. But the house hadn't been any worse than usual, and none of the coordinators had been in trouble lately. I didn't think I had anything to worry about.

Al took another sip of his coffee and then spoke in a voice that was a yell.

"Bring in Rossen."

Thirty-four people finally exhaled.

Evelyn stood up and hurried out the back door. Al was settling back down onto his perch on the window ledge when Evelyn returned through the back door, followed by Rossen and his P.O. Al stood up.

"Jake Rossen," he shouted. "Come on down!"

Jake walked to the front of the room smirking, hands in the pockets of the shorts that he wore over his long johns, his flapping, laceless shoes leaving dirty snow puddle tracks on the dining room floor. He stood before us with that peculiar look that only a teenager can effectively use; a look of detached innocence that's just insincere enough to allow the contempt and derision beneath it to shine through. If it bothered Al, he didn't show it. He started speaking as though Rossen wasn't even there.

"What makes Concept different is that we're not a detention center," Al began. "We don't care who you know on the street. It doesn't get you anything here. We don't care about what you've done in the past. It doesn't impress us. We *expect* you to help out the people in your house by booking incidents on them when they break the rules. If you have a contract with somebody, we break it, because we know that the only way for you to become men and women is to look at yourself honestly, and you can't be honest if you're sneaking around. Rats sneak around—men and women walk tall. And when you book an incident on someone—when you *help* them—you are rewarded. You don't have to worry about some punk sticking a shiv in your back, because this ain't juvie. If you act out physically, we don't call a code yellow and put you in leather restraints and shoot you full of Thorazine or Mellaril and leave you on a bed for ten hours until you calm down, because this ain't a mental hospital—this is Concept. We know what the people in detention centers and mental hospitals don't know—that you're not crazy—you're just *assholes*."

Al paused while everybody laughed. Everybody except Rossen.

"You were sent here because all those places didn't work. You knew how to get over on those people. You knew how to manipulate them, to tell them what they wanted to hear. And now this is your last chance. Most of you are doing your best. You work hard, you use your groups, you do everything you need to in order to move up the hierarchy and become an adult."

He paused to stub out his cigarette on the ashtray on the ledge.

"We have four staff members," he continued. "We don't run this house. *You* run this house. We're here to make sure you get what you need. We make sure you go to school, that you have beds to sleep in, that you get three meals a day, and that you have your sundries, your toothbrushes and soap. If you're sick, there's a nurse on duty. If you need clothes, we get your parents or guardians or the state to get them to you. But what you *really* need is the help of your peers. We can't give that to you. And the only way your peers can help you is if this house is free of violence. You can't be helped if you're living in fear."

He shook a fresh Merit out of the pack and walked over to stand next to Rossen.

"I've been doing this for *thirteen* years," he said, tapping the bottom of the cigarette filter with his index finger. He said that during every G.M. We were four days away from the new year—I wondered if he'd remember to start saying fourteen.

"Concept saved my life," he continued, "and I've seen it save hundreds of lives since then. *And that's why I get so pissed off when some fucking punk comes into my house and tries to turn it into a fucking prison! Does anybody have any feelings for this asshole?*"

A sea of bodies swarmed Jake. We screamed at him for a full five minutes, standing inches from his face, which was soon covered in flecks of saliva. He never stopped smirking. Jake had been G.M.'d so many times he was practically immune.

"Since you like throwing chairs," said Al when the last of us had sat back down, "we're gonna put you in the main event."

Jake sneered at him. "I threw it at a window, not at my P.O."

Al ignored him and lit his cigarette.

Matthew spoke up.

"Everybody get up and make a ring."

We moved to the front of the room and formed a human ring around Jake. Matthew pulled a pair of shoelaces from his pocket and handed them to Jake, who began lacing up his sneakers. Carr entered the ring, followed by DeJong, who was carrying two pairs of red boxing gloves.

DeJong helped Carr get his gloves on while Matthew helped Jake. When they were ready, Al checked the gloves to make sure they were on tight. He stepped out of the ring, and Matthew took off his watch. He hit the button on the side of the watch, and said, "Fight."

Carr and Rossen circled each other, Carr throwing an occasional jab, and Rossen deflecting it easily. Usually when guys were in the ring, fists started flying right away. These guys were sizing each other up. Carr threw another jab and Rossen batted it away, laughing in that sneering way of his. Carr threw a hard straight but Rossen side-stepped it and Sean almost fell over.

"What's the matter, ass-kiss?" said Rossen. Then the fight was on. Carr jabbed a few times and landed a haymaker to the nose. Jab, jab, jab, punch. He did it again—jab, jab, jab, punch. And again. Rossen couldn't time him; he kept getting caught defending the jab and leaving his nose wide open. After the fourth big punch had landed, Rossen was bleeding. He grabbed Carr around the shoulders and threw a few weak punches at the back of his head.

Matthew yelled "Break!" and stepped in to pry them apart. As soon as Matthew stepped out of the way, Rossen threw a punch right at the front of Carr's sweatpants. Carr moved and it must've caught him in the lower belly because instead of keeling over, he just lurched to his left and threw a wild haymaker that missed its mark before he righted himself.

The crowd was loving it, cheering Sean on and erupting every time he landed a punch. There was less circling and jabbing now, and more sudden rushes and wild, violent swings. Whenever either guy came too close to the edge of the ring, either by backing away or getting knocked into us, we'd shove him back toward the center.

Rossen started getting his bearings and he was landing solid straight rights to Carr's jaw. Carr, instead of deflecting the blows, was going toe to toe; he was giving as good as he was getting but he was getting hit hard.

"Time!"

Matthew stepped into the ring and separated the guys. I pulled a chair out for Carr. Rossen had to stand. He put his glove under his shirt and lifted it to wipe away the blood trickling from his nose. Carr sat down puffing but did his best to look like he wasn't winded. The left side of his jaw was red from the mouth to the jawline, like he had been hit with a brick. I would have given him advice, but I didn't know anything about fighting. Dave Vazquez, a big bull of a guy who had been an amateur boxer in New Jersey, was crouched in front of Carr, stuttering away in his face.

"He c-c-can't take it in the b-b-belly. H-h-hit him d-d-downstairs!"

"Yeah, okay," said Carr.

"H-h-he's not j-j-jabbing. W-w-when he throws a straight, g-g-go for the upperc-c-cut."

Carr didn't have time to answer as Matthew was calling them back to the center of the ring. Al stood to the left of the ring looking on uninterestedly, as if his part in the ring was only a formality.

The second round started. Carr didn't listen to Vazquez's advice as far as I could tell. He kept rushing Rossen or letting Rossen rush him, then they'd trade shots until one of them clinched or backed off. Carr got a few good shots in at Rossen's nose, but he spent most of the round taking shots to the left side of his face and trying to push Rossen away.

When Carr sat back down in the chair, his lip was starting to blow up and he had the beginning of a black eye. He was puffing a lot harder and his face was dripping with sweat. Vazquez gave him more advice, which he swore to take.

"Had enough, Jake?" asked Al. Rossen was wounded, but like Carr he was doing his best to look like this was all a minor annoyance.

"Hell no," answered Jake. "I'm winning."

The crowd booed this comment and laughed at him, but anybody could see he was holding his own. He wasn't doing as well as his Charles Bronson demeanor would suggest, but he'd had the upper hand in the second round. Al didn't want to believe it, and neither did I, but Carr was in worse shape.

Matthew called them back to the ring and Rossen went into a half crouch before Matthew had moved away from them. As Matthew backed off, Rossen came up and rang Carr's bell with a haymaker. For the next sixty seconds, it looked like Rossen might knock Carr out. He threw a flurry of punches and all Carr could do was try to block them. In the first two rounds both guys had been throwing nothing but hard rights; Carr only used his left to jab. Now Rossen was throwing straights with his right and hooks with his left and he was beating the hell out of Carr. But eventually he tired out, and he was faced with a very pissed-off Carr. Carr's face was red with embarrassment and anger and as Rossen stepped back and put his hands up, Carr rushed him.

Rossen wasn't very good at defending himself. Carr's punches were big and slow but he was connecting with Rossen's face more times than not. Jake kept stepping back, but the crowd kept pushing him forward; inevitably he was pushed into a fist.

When Matthew called time, they both stood exhausted and bleeding. Al moved into the ring.

"You're not so tough after all, Jake." He looked at Jake but he was really speaking to us. "There's always somebody tougher than you, and in Concept, if you make us prove it, we prove it. You sure don't look too dangerous now." The crowd roared its approval.

"He didn't beat me," said Rossen. His curly black hair was matted down on his forehead with sweat. "I'll take him in the next round."

"You were *beat,* Jake," answered Al. He said it authoritatively but you only had to look in his eyes to see what he really thought. He just wanted this to be over and all it would take was for Jake to back down.

"He didn't beat me," Jake repeated. There was something about the way he said it. He didn't say it in his typical arrogant way. He said it like it was an obvious fact that anybody could see. And the problem was, we *did* all see it. If Al had polled us, we all would've said that Carr had creamed him. But I don't think any of us believed it. And Al knew it. Rossen wasn't winning by much, but he *was* winning.

"You wanna keep going, Jake?" Al's eyes had changed. He was all business now. When Al got this look it was a lot scarier than when he got pissed off, because there was no understanding at all in this look; it was the look of a guy who's no longer really in control of a situation but has no choice but to behave as if he is.

"Yeah, I'll keep going," Rossen said with a smug, crooked smile. He glanced over at Carr. "It won't take too much longer."

Al raised his eyebrows in exaggerated innocent surprise.

"Oh, no. No. Sean is done for the day." Carr looked a little irritated at being dismissed from the ring, but he looked a little relieved as well. "You're pretty confident," Al

continued, "so we're going to oblige you with a challenge."
He paused. "How about Vazquez?"

Vazquez's eyes lit up. "I'll f-f-fight," he said. It wasn't
that he was eager to hurt anybody—Vazquez was actually a
very gentle guy—it was just that he liked boxing. But he
had about five inches and forty pounds on Rossen.

"Do you need sweats?" asked Al.

Vazquez was in his Levi's. "I-I-I'm o-k-k-kay like this,"
he said.

"This is bullshit," said Rossen. He was right, but I
couldn't help enjoying the fact that his usually cocky demeanor had been replaced by an aura of abject fear; he was
making a terrific effort to look calm but his eyes were los-
ing the battle.

"Not at all," said Al. "You wanna live by prison rules,
then live by 'em. Rule one is that might is right. If this were
really a prison, you would've been somebody's punk on
your first day. As it is, we're just giving you what you asked
for."

Matthew finished helping Vazquez into the gloves and
he called for them to fight as he and Al stepped out of the
ring. The crowd was really worked up, screaming for
Vazquez to get him. Rossen tried to put his hands up to
protect himself but Vazquez stepped up to him and pushed
them away with his left hand and jabbed him a few times.
Rossen put his hands back up and shot a right out at
Vazquez's belly. Vazquez took the punch without moving
and pushed Rossen back against the crowd. We pushed
him back toward the ring just to get him off them, but
Vazquez was pushing against Rossen's chest with his left

hand and pounding his face with the right. I counted the punches; there were nine of them, and that doesn't sound like a lot, but when you can't move and a guy's hitting you that hard at close range, it's more than enough. Somebody was screaming, "Kill the punk!" and I heard somebody shouting "Holy shit!" over and over as Vazquez pummeled Rossen. By the last punch, Rossen was already falling; as Vazquez stepped away, Jake slumped to one knee. I don't know if he really knew where he was. His nose was shattered and the lower half of his face was a mask of blood. Al called a couple of expeditors over to take Rossen to the nurse.

The G.M. simply ended after Rossen left the room. Al didn't say anything about the beating. He just told me to get my crew to get lunch ready and he left the room.

Jake Rossen was taken to the hospital with a broken nose. He never came back to Concept. I heard that his folks pulled him out, but then somebody else told me that they'd run out of money. I heard a few weeks later that he was in some other place—more like a mental hospital—in Florida. Which seemed appropriate, I guess, given the craziness of Concept itself.

As for me, I kept having my ups and downs. Maybe more downs than ups. When the money from the state was about to run out, the staff started giving me promotions a lot more quickly. They always tried to avoid kicking people out. Kicking somebody out meant you were giving hope to everybody else. Graduation looked better to everybody— the residents, the staff, the state agencies and psychiatrists that sent kids to Concept. Graduation meant Concept *worked*. So they didn't push me too hard on the small things, and I graduated at twenty-one months. I know Concept worked for some people. I guess it did for me, too; I'm pushing forty and my adventures with drugs are limited to a couple of beers on the weekends and a few Tylenols when I get a headache. Maybe I would've cooled down anyway, I don't know. But I haven't forgotten Concept. I don't think I ever will.

See Ya

Terry Quinn

For the seventeen minutes it takes a goddam
Lower East Side ambulance not to come
to the war zone where she's put in a hitch
and seen plenty, Jesus, tons of stuff she can use
If not now then later, Monica the gonna-be novelist
watches ultra hard as a neighbor she's yet to meet
becomes a corpse. Her first.

And all over the usual powder, she bets.
It lies around him like an aura. No,
like a hem for the blue flesh of his body.
Blue with cold and last aloneness—
except for the ragged hole in his neck.
And that a black-red fountain not just spurting,

bubbling, flowing wild but draining somehow color
from the pupils of his eyes.

Here's why Monica knows it's time to move.
Not because she might be next. In Albuquerque
she might be next. And not because she's scared
either at feeling zero sympathy for this man—
himself a murderous geek if ever she's seen one.
It's that her hunger has finally ended by making her
root for death. Making her hope for calamity here
beyond a hackneyed wounding.

And if it were a so-so friend, an acquaintance say,
twitching on the bottom three steps of her stoop,
would that . . . would Monica . . .
All ears for a siren whine, she wonders what she'll
take from Avenue B. Anything she brought there,
For example?

The Heart Finds Its Own Conclusion

Manuel Muñoz

There was more to it than a woman with long black hair, flipped high in front, a woman wearing just pink panties low on the hip, her hands on a sheer curtain, a woman looking out of a window, down into the street. Cecilia wished she could remember the face of the man who had just left the room, who had closed the door after himself, and the woman who had put her hand against it as if the door had captured his warmth. But that had been years ago, back when Cecilia had been a child, and the actress with the long black hair had never become famous. That woman couldn't be easily found and identified. She wasn't Mia Farrow with her shorn hair in *Rosemary's Baby*. She wasn't Jane Fonda with her voice crackling ominously over the radio from North Vietnam. The film, too, had been forgettable: a drug-running movie from the 1970s, set somewhere in a dusty outpost in Mexico. Cecilia remembered nothing of it but glimpses: the cars like the woman's hair—long and black—with windows tinted against the sun baking the roads; men with guns shooting for the glory of the sound; a fat man being lifted away from a room, a squealer who had faced his revenge, his white shirt bloody and upraised to show the full expanse of his belly; the cars giving chase to one another, careening past potholes and kicking up dust, bouncing and jostling like their old family car, the give-and-take of the weak suspension. But the story, the how of that woman. What she saw when she looked out of the window, the dank, tiny room with an even tinier bed, a bed she had shared passionately with the man who had just left her. Cecilia didn't remember that: that had been when Tía Sara had covered her eyes, *tsk-tsk-tsk* between her teeth. A dank, tiny room with a single washbasin jutting out of the wall, a mirror where the woman could have washed her face and looked up at herself to discover her own longing. That, though, Cecilia only invented. There was nothing but a room, a departed man, and a woman in pink panties with long black hair.

Over there was the Crest Theater—the *cine*—its once grand, sparkly marquee where Tío Nico and Tía Sara would take them to see movies. The marquee stood bare now, the lights off. Those years ago, the *cine* had been no place for children, but there they had been, Cecilia and her cousin Sergio being herded toward the flashing neon. Cecilia had held on to Tío Nico's hand as the woman behind the small ticket booth spoke into the speaker box. The booth stood at the edge of the *cine's* facade, the marquee twinkling bright above the long, sloping entrance to the doors. Her booth shone warm and bright, room enough just for her stool, and she slipped tickets through the mouse hole in the glass. Cecilia still remembered all of it: the shiny tiles of the *cine* entrance; the click-click of Tía Sara as she edged to the doors, then the quiet carpet once they got inside; the *aguas frescas* bubbling in their fountains; the Mexican candy with a scarlet rose on the wrapper; the tall stacks of paper cups, swirled in purple and green; the length of the lobby and the ladies waiting patiently outside the bathroom door; the slender wooden phone booths and a man getting inside one, sliding the door against the crowd, a light turning on so he could see; the waft of sauerkraut and mustard and jalapeños from the side counter; the whirr of the ice cream machine; the door to one of the theaters opening and tinny voices coming through like caught conversation.

She could see the *cine* from where she was parked, as close as possible to the front doors of the bus station in Fresno. She'd driven a long way to pick up her cousin Sergio, who had called her at work late in the afternoon. Since her desk at the insurance office was right next to her boss's front door, Cecilia had urged Sergio off the phone with a quick approval, even though getting to Fresno meant at least half an hour of driving. When the six o'clock bus from Bakersfield arrived, Sergio hadn't been on it.

It was February and dark by six o'clock. There, on the south side of Fresno, on the fringe of downtown that emptied after dark, there wasn't much except vacant parking lots and very dark spaces. Cecilia was frightened of Fresno these days, how Fresno got to be like this, all big-city trouble and worry. Every day in the break room at work, Cecilia read the newspaper and there was always some terrible story coming out of the city. Gas station holdups with stabbed clerks; teenage boys getting guns from who knows where. She knew danger, the difference between accident and deliberate harm, the difference between the trouble in the city and the tragedies of everyday life in towns as small as hers. At the insurance office, Cecilia filed all the initial slips for the month's claims and witnessed the peril in everything. A house fire in Selma; an old man slipped in the tub, now on his way to a rest home in Parlier; a school beating more brutal than usual in Visalia; car wrecks all along the too-thin roads dissecting the county; farm machinery accidents she wished she had never read about. A despondent farmer who had come in to tell about a group of kids with matches sending his barn up in flames, then having to race down one of his badly burned hogs to shoot it out of its misery.

"I really have to get out of here," Sergio had said and Cecilia heard what she thought was desperation. "I'm going whether you help me or not, Cecilia, so come get me. Please."

Sergio lived with Tía Sara in Bakersfield and this was what bad blood meant: Cecilia was now twenty-three years old and she had been raised by Tío Nico and Tía Sara after her own parents were killed in a train accident in Mexico. Bad blood meant that when Tío Nico and Tía Sara divorced, Tía Sara took Sergio to Bakersfield to raise him under strict religion. Tío Nico kept Cecilia because she was his brother's daughter and blood meant something to him. Both sides had done their best to turn the two cousins against each other, but Cecilia had always known better. To help Sergio, she would have to lie to Tío Nico, but that was fine—the problems he had with Tía Sara were between the two of them.

How bad it was that Sergio had to leave, Cecilia didn't know, even though he should have moved out and gotten a job when he graduated from high school two years ago. How bad it was that his voice shook with worry when he called her, Cecilia couldn't say. She had heard it catching his voice over the phone. She had never heard him sound like that and that was enough to bring her here.

Cecilia could hear Highway 99 off in the distance, even with the windows sealed up. All around downtown Fresno were its signatures: on-ramps and off-ramps, the road signs that glared bright with reflection, the stark stretch of overpasses and the starker worlds underneath them. The six o'clock bus, empty now, departed along a side street. Three taxis lined up to take away the few standing passengers. The station stood quiet once again. Cecilia could see the clerk behind the long desk, dressed in his blue uniform and hat, reading the paper, and she watched him for a little bit, hoping he would reach for the phone or the radio to hear about another bus coming late. But he was as still as the empty streets around the station.

Over that way were the new county offices where Tío

Nico cleaned. He told Cecilia that he left promptly at five o'clock during winter because the downtown area was so dangerous. He would be dismayed if he knew that she was here, waiting for Sergio. *"Bueno pa' nada,"* she could hear Tío Nico say. "Not worth a damn thing, and he's a drain on you. He knows you've got a job and that's all he cares about." It was difficult sometimes for Cecilia to reconcile that Tío Nico was talking about his own child—though they were cousins, she could not think of Sergio as anything but a brother. After all, Sergio himself called his father Tío Nico. Cecilia could never refuse him. She wasn't at all like her aunt or uncle, before or after they separated.

She tapped her fingers on the steering wheel, impatient. The station clerk nodded off behind the glass. It wasn't anywhere near late, but in this part of Fresno, with its quiet streets, the hour seemed deep into the night, the buildings around her glimmering halfheartedly. A taxi prowled by, but seeing no one on the sidewalk, sped off in the direction of the train station, which was newer and better lit.

In the old days, before the new train station, the buses brought everyone in. Cecilia remembered clearly the amount of traffic over in this direction on the nights they went to the Crest. All those years past, the adults so careful in spite of the glory and brightness of the neon, the packed parking lot and the families milling out, the long line snaking away from the ticket booth. The buses brought wave after wave of workers from Los Angeles and San Diego. Barbershops and shoe stores waited over in the Fulton Mall with doors open and inviting, just walking distance away, where the men suited up in cowboy hats and new Wrangler jeans if they had the money, the smell of their new haircuts gently wafting down the dark aisles of the theater. Back then, things were grander. Cecilia didn't know how those men made a living, how they managed to find a place to stay, only that they showed up in nicely pressed shirts and held open the doors for the ladies every chance they had. Now, just the parking lots with cracked asphalt, potholes, muddy patches, and sagging fences, all the lights gone dark and dangerous.

A car was coming down the street, rolling slowly, and Cecilia could see the driver scanning the sidewalk. It was a black car, something from the late eighties, a Cutlass maybe, if she remembered correctly from filing so many insurance claims. The car was coming in her direction, slowing down even more, and she did her best not to look in the driver's direction. But she couldn't help herself, with the driver having rolled down his window to the cold February night air, and when the car passed, Cecilia looked over and the man behind the wheel stared back.

Her heart raced. Those forms she filed, those stories she read. You give the teenage boys the money they want. You don't ever go to a service station after nine o'clock. You don't let the kid ride with you on the jumpy seat of a tractor, no matter how slow it's going. You look in every direction before you enter the intersection and you let the rain and fog slow you down. Yet here was the car turning around and pulling up right behind her, the headlights on and the man's silhouette rigid in the driver's seat. He idled the engine for only a moment before he turned it off and his headlights turned out as well, sending Cecilia's car back into a dark deeper than she thought she'd been in.

She put her hand on the ignition and waited. Over in that bus station, she could see the clerk still nodding in sleep. Her heart raced, raced as it had in the days of the Crest *cine,* just right over there, where the woman with the long black hair had stood at the window as her hands lovingly stroked the curtain when a knock at the door made her turn around. The woman had walked over, the sound of high heels amplified—yes, only panties and high heels. The hoots started from the men in the back row. The woman had opened the door and two men immediately forced their way into the room, demanding to know where her lover had gone. The whistles from the back row grew fiercer still, Tía Sara's *tsk-tsk-tsk* ever sharper, and her thick hand tried to shield Cecilia's eyes. But Tía Sara had been just as engrossed in the story as the men in the back row and she had been concerned for this woman in the face of menace. Her aunt's thick hand had loosened and Cecilia saw the two thugs begin to rough up the woman. The men had whistled louder as the woman screamed her denials. Cecilia remembered her gigantic, round breasts, the deep swollen purple of the nipples, the way the thugs brushed their hands against them. Cecilia had wanted love to come back into the room, for the woman's man to return and save her. Her heart had raced and raced, set in its own belief that any moment the man would come back.

Cecilia heard the car door open, and the silhouette stepped out. She watched the man nonchalantly begin his walk to the station, his footsteps echoing against the sidewalk. Cecilia leaned in to press the horn full-force just in case. As he passed her car, he leaned down a bit to look inside and caught her glance.

"Hey," he shouted so she could hear him through the window. "You his sister?"

She turned the ignition.

"Hey!" the man shouted. "Hey!" He jumped in front of her car and tapped hard on the hood. "You his sister? Are you Sergio's sister?"

Cecilia had not turned on the headlights and so she could not see his face clearly. Through his winter coat, his shoulders stretched powerfully and explained his fearlessness, his hands still on the hood and him standing right in front of her car.

"You don't need to be scared of me," he said, shaking his head. "I came for your brother." He lifted his hands from the hood, as if in surrender, and pointed to the bus station. "In there? You want to come in there?"

He began walking toward the station, where the clerk was still asleep. He walked toward it, but still faced her, waving her in his direction, encouraging. The sound of his footsteps receded, a fainter clicking against the sidewalk, and it reminded her of the woman in the movie and her high heels, how the sound wasn't matching exactly with the precision of her steps. Cecilia lost herself watching the man get closer and closer to the door—he was wearing boots, some kind of dark shoes with a heel, and his winter coat reached past his waist. The lobby gleamed in its fluorescent light and safety: She could rattle on the clerk's window if she had to.

She turned off the ignition and gathered herself. Her keys in a tight fist, purse crooked in her elbow, Cecilia stepped out of the car. She crossed her arms against the cold and half-ran to the door, keeping her eyes fixed on the clerk behind the glass. The lonely drone of Highway 99, off in the distance, filtered through the empty parking lots and into the streets, the wire fences slouched and creaking. She rushed even faster as she got closer to the door, almost running inside, the doors banging heavily back into place, the sound echoing in the empty lobby. The clerk, though, made no motion. He slept behind the cloudy partition to his booth, the thick pane scratched with large gashes.

The man was sitting on one of the orange plastic benches. He had taken off his coat and he was powerful, his shoulders massive and round. He was older than her, older than Sergio, maybe in his late twenties but she couldn't tell for sure. He sat leaning forward, elbows on his knees and arms extended out, legs spread wide, claiming space. She caught the glimmer of a thin gold chain around his neck, his hands clean of rings, hair cropped so short the scalp showed, a goatee busy around his chin. She hadn't seen that in the dark.

"So you're his sister," he said.

She didn't move. "I'm his cousin, not his sister."

"Well, that's what he told me," the man said.

The clerk finally stirred in the booth and, seeing her standing in front of the partition, sighed heavily and sat up straight.

"Cecilia, right?" he asked, but when she wouldn't

answer, he rolled his eyes. "What? Are you a Bible thumper like your mom? That woman rags on me something hard. Do I look like a bad guy to you?"

"Yeah, I'm Cecilia," she said. She felt caught, having to admit this. He was talking about Tía Sara; he had somehow been at the house in Bakersfield. She turned slowly to the station doors as if to check for the next bus, but it was embarrassment and nerves and shame that made her want to turn away from this man. She didn't know how to ask him who he was.

He seemed to know. "Sergio ever mention me?" He waited for her to speak. "Huh? Sergio ever mention me?"

From the doors, her car was farther away than she thought. On one of the opposite corners, Cecilia glimpsed a woman waiting to cross the street, hand on her hip. Even from here, she could tell the woman was wearing a short skirt and heels, impervious to the cold, heading in the direction of the old Chinatown a few blocks over, where all the prostitutes congregated. She scanned the horizon, looked over at the Crest, its dark arch barely visible.

"He has something of mine," the man said.

With that she turned to look at him. "Who are you?" she finally demanded. "Sergio called me to come pick him up, not you."

"You don't know me?" His voice pitched higher, edging toward frustration, maybe anger. "You don't know who I am?"

"No," she said, finally giving in. "I don't."

"He's got my heart," the man said, melodramatically

holding his hands across his chest, but he sneered a bit when he said it. "He's got a lot of things I want back."

Cecilia stared at him, that goatee, that way of sitting that had grown into an arrogant posture, that sound in his insistent questions, the size of his shoulders, and his shorn head. She could picture this man laughing at Tía Sara. She wanted to speak sharply to him, but she knew she would have Tía Sara's voice—powerless, no matter what the anger and vehemence. Tía Sara's voice, back when they were children, fell up against Tío Nico's louder, more voracious yelling and drowned in his heaviness, the way his voice penetrated the walls. Tío Nico's voice was like the men who had catcalled in the darkness of the Crest *cine,* right over there, all of the men in the back row with their newly shined shoes and slicked-back hair, their voices rising to a slur of cheer and whistle, so loud it was impossible to hear what the woman with long black hair had wanted to say in protest. The woman had wanted the two thugs at the door to go away, to stop harassing her, but the men in the theater somehow urged them on.

"You look just like him, Cecilia," the man said to her and she remembered then how Sergio's voice had shook with worry on the phone. "He's a pretty little bitch."

"Jesus . . ." she muttered. Because of the empty street, she knocked on the clerk's booth, rapped her knuckles on the scratched partition as if he were still sleeping. "When's the next bus?" she demanded.

The clerk was about Sergio's age, dark-skinned and gangly with a head of thick, uncombed hair. When he stood up, she could see that his uniform shirt was too big for him and that he wasn't wearing a belt. His pants drooped down past his hips. He reached over impatiently for a clipboard, eyeing Cecilia.

"The seven o'clock," he told her. He had a little speaker vent in the partition like the one at the booth for the Crest. "It stops in Goshen and Tulare before this."

"Is it going to be late?"

"Schedule says seven o'clock."

"That's not what I asked you," Cecilia told him gruffly. "Is it going to be late?"

"They're on time."

"Can you radio or something?"

"Nah, I can't." She could tell he was lying, but it wasn't worth the trouble. The clerk deserved none of her nervous anger, none of her confusion as she struggled to come up with a reason behind Sergio's phone call, his fleeing, and now this man sitting in the lobby waiting for him.

"You want to follow me to Goshen?" the man asked her. She heard him stand up, his boots sounding against the lobby floor, the footfalls slow and patient and coming toward her.

Cecilia didn't want to answer him anymore. She didn't want to speak another word to him, but she could do nothing but wait and stare outside again, standing by the doors of the bus station and the clerk who had gone back to his own idle business. The man's footsteps came closer and closer and when they stopped, she didn't have to turn around to know that he was there behind her. She folded her arms against herself, against the anticipation of having him touch her and the lanky boy behind the counter not knowing what to do if he did.

"Suit yourself, then," the man said and he brushed past her, pushed himself through the lobby doors and into the night air. He stood on the sidewalk, facing the street and not turning around.

By the station clock, the next bus would be arriving shortly. There would be no time to race down to Goshen, a little town with nothing but a bus station open after dark, a little town more dark and quiet than this part of Fresno. Sergio would not think to get off in Goshen. If he would have seen her car there, he might have, glad to see his cousin, and Cecilia cursed herself for not having thought of it sooner. But there had been no way of knowing. There had been only Sergio's voice and the passing, fleeting sigh she had made on the phone, her resignation at his supposed despair. There may have been worry in his voice, but Cecilia's imagination had led her no further than Tía Sara's open Bible, her old hands steadying on a choice line. There had been no way of knowing, of preparing for possibilities, of finding a way to prevent consequences. If only Sergio had mentioned this man waiting out on the sidewalk, then maybe she could have gone home and pleaded with Tío Nico to come to Fresno with her, because strange men were always dangerous.

Over along the wall was a bank of telephones and Cecilia searched in her coat for coins. She shook her purse hoping to hear the tiny scatter of loose change but there was nothing or not enough, so she dialed the operator and gave the woman the number to Tía Sara's house in Bakersfield.

"Tía, it's me, Celi," she said loudly, as if the operator were deliberately taking her time and then her aunt's voice came over the line, timid in its confusion.

"Celi? Celi?"

"Tía, I'm at the bus station in Fresno. Sergio told me to come get him." She turned to look outside, where the man was still standing on the sidewalk, his impatient hands in his coat pockets.

"*Ay, Dios mio,* Sergio," her aunt said. "Celi bring him back here to me."

"Tía, there's a man here waiting for him."

"*Ay,*" she said, again, but this time it came as a near sob, as something said with her hand on her forehead, the anguish overcoming her so much that she couldn't say any more.

"Tía, please. Who is he?"

"He's been running with a bad crowd, *m'ija.* I don't know what Sergio has gotten himself into these days, why he's like this. That man is terrible. He's the devil. . . ."

Cecilia had to pull the receiver away from her ear, laying it close to the top of her shoulder and closing her eyes, wishing it could be simple: Who was the man and how did Sergio know him and why was he running and why hadn't Tía Sara overcome her lifelong rage and simply called Tío Nico's house, admitted that there was trouble and that she could not handle it herself. Her aunt's voice flowed on, incessant, onto her shoulder, but she knew her aunt could tell her nothing.

"Tía," she said, interrupting her only to realize that Tía Sara had already started sobbing. She listened to her tears over the static in the line. "Tía," she said again, hoping she would collect herself.

"Pray with me," Tía Sara told her, sniffling, and she could almost hear the pages of her old Bible turning in her lap, the big Bible with the red dye across the top. "Please pray with me, that Sergio knows this is a house of love."

"He knows that, Tía." She sighed. "I'll bring him home."

"Please, Celi. You remember, don't you? From *Primer Corintios*. Recite with me," she pleaded. "You remember. 'Love is patient . . .'"

"'Love is kind,'" she had to say, because Tía Sara had paused, her tears on the brink of starting again and Cecilia could not bear to hear them. She knew what was behind them, every time Tía Sara wept like this, the agony of having made the wrong decision years and years ago, having left Tío Nico, having split the children up as they did, the troubles with Sergio only pointing to her as a failure.

"'It always protects,'" her aunt recited softly. "'It always trusts.'"

Even from the bank of telephones, Cecilia could hear the bus approaching, the chug of its engine from down the street. "It's here," she told her aunt, who was still reciting. "I have to go, Tía. Sergio's here." She hung up the receiver with Tía Sara still in midprayer and rushed over to the doors, where the bus had pulled up alongside the curb, its brakes tightening and releasing in a hiss, exhausted. The man inched closer to the front of the bus, waiting for the door to pop open. From behind the dark, tinted windows, silhouettes rose from their seats on the bus and gathered in single file to disembark.

The driver got out first, an older man like Tío Nico, his face framed by giant glasses, a graying mustache. He came down lithely, a vigor in his step, and he stood at the bus's foothold, his arm extended out at the man waiting for Sergio as if to bar him from approaching. He was letting the passengers exit and they came forth in a steady stream—men just like the ones Cecilia saw years and years ago, still coming, still arriving with nothing on them but a wallet of emergency money. They stepped off one by one and whenever a woman approached her descent, the old driver extended his hand graciously to her, helped the inevitable children being towed along. The sidewalk gradually crowded, the passengers pushing back even the man waiting for Sergio. There was luggage in the bins of the bus's underbelly. There were cars coming now, out of nowhere, waiting across the street, people coming out of them and collecting their long-awaited arrivals. There was such a sudden cacophony of voices, something disarming about this amount of activity, and it made Cecilia feel safe. She stepped out of the lobby to the loud sighing of the bus in idle, of cigarettes being lit in relief, keeping her eyes on the line of silhouettes still on the bus. Taxis pulled up as if summoned and the cabmen opened their doors and waved people over, crying out, "Anywhere! Anywhere! Five bucks!"

She saw Sergio, her cousin, her brother, step down out of the bus, a grocery sack under his arm. There were clothes in that sack—there had to be—how Tía Sara had run off in the initial days, stuffing what she could in a large paper bag and dragging Sergio with her. How ridiculous, Cecilia thought immediately, how it must have signaled that the gesture was nothing but dramatics and flourish. It was all for show, all for presenting to the waiting relative who offered the warm bed: This was all they could bring with them, all they had time to bring.

But just as she was about to raise her hand to Sergio and wave him over, to get them in the car and admonish him—just a little bit—for such unnecessary worry, Sergio saw the man waiting for him and the look on his face sank into terror. He began to push his way past some of the other passengers, but the man rushed at him and caught Sergio by the shoulder, enveloping him, his face scowling.

"You little fucker—you think I didn't know you'd come here?" The man hit Sergio hard against the back of his head, his palm flat and backed by the force of his rolling shoulders, and Sergio's hands reached up to feel the spot, to ward off another blow. His hands were working on reflex, Cecilia knew, and he let out a shocked grunt that caught the attention of everyone surrounding them. The women with their children brought the little hands closer, not knowing what to do because their luggage was still in the underbelly of the bus. The men did nothing but watch.

"Sergio!" she called out, moving to them, but the man hit him again and Sergio dropped the grocery bag. One of the men absently picked it up and held it out to Sergio, as if ignoring what was actually happening.

"Celi," Sergio said, finally seeing her. "Just stay out of it." Tears had started in his eyes and he took the grocery sack from the passenger holding it out to him, wiping at his nose. The man handled him gruffly by the arm, hand gripped right under Sergio's armpit and lifting him past the passengers, heading toward the black car. Cecilia started after them.

"Didn't you fucking hear him?" the man called back at her. "Stay out of it, you fucking bitch!" he shouted, so loud, as if signaling the men from the bus not to interfere, and they made no motion to help Cecilia.

"Llame a la policia," one of the women whispered, so quiet.

He shoved Sergio in the passenger seat, Cecilia still looking on and unable to move, and she began to cry, watching Sergio wide-eyed in the car, his head hanging down. "Sergio!" she called out and the same woman spoke up a little more, her voice more insistent: the police, the police, but it was happening too fast for her. Sergio made no motion to get out of the car and run—to what?—even as the man slammed the passenger door and walked around to the other side. He turned around to glare at her, keeping his eyes unblinking and stern as he started the car, and then he sped down the street.

The passengers around Cecilia stared at her indecision. The women with children rushed to get their luggage, looking impatiently for their rides, and Cecilia knew what they were thinking. The escalation of arguments, the return of that man, maybe a gun and shots being fired. Hadn't they all seen stories like that? Hadn't they all witnessed what men could do when love was denied? Hadn't they all realized a man's way of loving, of loving what he could not have? The men from the bus began to walk away, uninterested, and Cecilia silently cursed them through her tears, how ineffectual they were, how their bravado was held in reserve when it really mattered.

The sidewalk was emptying. The old driver brought down the doors to the luggage bins, gently closing them back into place. Cecilia watched him because she did not know what else to do. The taxis began to drive away with passengers inside and some of them turned to look at her through the back windows, still standing there. The sidewalk would be bare soon and she knew better than to be standing there alone. There was nothing left to do.

The old driver came over to her. He was an older man, like Tío Nico, and the wrinkles in his face softened him, as did his gray mustache and the thick glasses. Faded and clouded like the panes of the clerk's lobby booth, the plastic lenses were from a state-aid program, Cecilia knew, the frames old and well-worn, but the man had been careful with them. He blinked hard at Cecilia, as if he were having a hard time seeing through to her.

"You okay, *mujercita*?" he asked, blinking at her as if hoping she would say yes.

"I'm fine," she answered.

"They did the same thing in Bakersfield. But that was in the afternoon, so there was a police officer." He kept staring at her, waiting for her to respond, but Cecilia had nothing left to say.

"Thank you," she said, absently, for lack of anything else.

"It's not like the old days," the old driver said. "People used to be a lot more civilized. People never acted like this."

He turned and eased up onto the first step of the bus.

He finally strained, showing his age, the long drive. "So sorry," he said, turning briefly, and then he closed the door and started up the bus. He pulled it away, going down the street, and leaving the front of the station quiet again.

She had to go now, before it became late, before the sidewalk was completely bare of people. She would have to tell Tío Nico, find a way to elicit some kind of sympathy for Sergio. She would have to ask him to call Tía Sara to find out what they could do. Tía Sara would do no such crying in front of Tío Nico. Tía Sara would put up a front of resilience and Cecilia counted on that.

Walking back to the car, holding her keys, she saw the glow of the Crest Theater over in the distance, its neon faint over the dead parking lots. Impossible, Cecilia thought, not after all these years. It could not be. It had to be a church housing itself in the old dusty seats. It had to be a real estate agency lighting the place in an attempt to promote the building. Not a movie, not even a Spanish-language film from these days.

Instead of heading in the direction of the highway, Cecilia drove the other way toward the theater, just to see, though it would take her deeper into downtown Fresno. The neon shone brighter as she approached it, not one letter absently unlit in the theater's name scrawled across the facade. But there was no one there, the booth empty and dark.

She idled the car at the intersection facing the theater and she saw herself being led out of the place by Tía Sara, those many years ago. She had begun crying in the middle of the movie, at what had happened to the woman with the long black hair. The two thugs had barged into the room and one of them closed the door. The other had clapped a hand over the woman's mouth when she began to scream. The men in the back of the theater whistled louder, the woman's large nipples purple in close-up, her legs straining to balance on her high heels. The single washbasin had a purpose then—one of the men turned the tap for a squeaky rush of water. They shouted questions at her, demanding again where her lover had gone, and when she wouldn't answer, the sink full now, the two men grabbed her head, her hand reaching up, as if by instinct, to stop them. Bent over the sink, breasts dangling, the backs of her thighs stretched in full view, the men in the theater cheered louder: *"¡Eso!"* "Right there!" *"¡Eso!"* The two thugs had begun drowning the woman in the pink panties and that had been when Cecilia rushed from her seat and bolted toward the lobby, the doors with the leather padding and small windows of light showing her the way out.

At twenty-three, Cecilia had not seen death personally. It had never made its presence known, not in the flesh, not in the immediacy of her everyday life. Her parents' death had come only as news, as something told to her many days after it had happened, as cold and clinical as the insurance claims she filed at work. She knew now that she still underestimated the fragility of life, that all (and everything) it meant was absence. But how did she know, back then when she was so young, that absence sprang from the spilling of blood? That absence began with a blow to the head, the rupture of skin, the throated cry, the body moving of its own accord, making some last gesture—it was the last she saw of the woman in the pink panties, her arm uselessly fending off the thugs, the men still cheering.

The intersection was deserted and Cecilia turned the car, suddenly frightened, suddenly fearful of not making it home in one piece. She checked the locks on the door. Even after the bare spaces of downtown Fresno, she had thirty miles of dark, lonely roads once she left the city, traveling all that distance before she made it back into the safe arms of Tío Nico, no matter what he thought of Sergio. Still, she knew, the terrified look in Sergio's eyes was a choice: He realized what had happened, how his plan had failed. That man without a name had a way of loving, his way of loving what he could not have, and it was not her place to say sorry. Sergio had stayed in the passenger seat, waiting for the man to drive him away, and her heart had to embrace Sergio's decision. It was like that woman's hand, her last desperate gesture—her body refused, gave way only by fighting, but her heart found its own conclusion, and it knew there would be no lover to come back and save it.

Fresno receded into a shimmering line in her rearview mirror. The February night broke only for her headlights, the dark fields around her where so many terrible things had happened to so many people. She would be home soon, crying into her uncle's shoulder, but now Cecilia wished, somehow, that it would be Tía Sara. Those many years ago, in the grace of the *cine*'s lobby, Tía Sara had bent down on one knee, bringing her in, her silk dress and the gentle scent of powder on her neck. The ladies lined up to use the bathroom, looking on, nodded their heads in sympathy. Cecilia wailed terribly and could not find enough consolation in Tía Sara's arms. The woman behind the counter came over with a fresh ice cream cone, holding it wrapped in a little paper napkin. The ladies kept looking on; some came over with tissues, with hard candy, their high heels sinking quietly into the carpet, so gentle.

An Interview with Yann Martel

Yann Martel's extraordinary novel Life of Pi *won the 2002 Man Booker Prize and was an international bestseller. It is the richly imagined story of a sixteen-year-old Indian boy named Pi Patel, a lover of stories and practitioner of many religions, who finds himself—the sole human survivor of a shipwreck— sharing a twenty-six foot lifeboat with a 450-pound Bengal tiger. How will he possibly survive? The answers are astonishing, and according to the* New York Times Book Review, "Life of Pi *could renew your faith in the ability of novelists to invest even the most outrageous scenario with plausible life."*

The following interview was conducted by e-mail with author Martel while he was living in Panama.

Q: How did this unusual novel begin?

A: It began like everything I've written. To start with there was the unconscious preparation, that state of permanent openness to new stories, to stories that will both move and make you think. I've been in that state of openness since the age of nineteen, when I started writing. After that—what came in through the open door—was the result of serendipity, inspiration, research, and hard work. The serendipity, in the case of *Life of Pi,* was a chance reading of a review in the *New York Times* of a Brazilian novel. The reviewer mentioned that in part of the novel the main character is stranded on a lifeboat in the company of a jaguar. That premise struck me. Noah's ark boiled down to one person and one animal—what perfect unity of time, place, and action. "Hmmm . . . I could do something with that," I thought. I inquired in a bookstore in Montreal about the book, *Max and the Cats,* by Moacyr Scliar. They didn't have it. Oh well. I forgot about it and wrote my first novel and life moved on.

Then, seven years later, I was in India at a dead end. A novel I was supposed to be writing was stillborn. I was quite depressed about it. I was in a hill station called Matheran, a few hours east of Bombay, and I was sitting on a boulder, looking down on the hot plains of Maharastra. Suddenly, out of nowhere—or, rather, from the creative ether of my unconscious—that premise, of someone stranded on a lifeboat with a wild animal, popped into my head. India and a lifeboat came together in my mind and there was an alchemical click. In the following exultant minutes, *Life of Pi*—all of it, the animals, the zoo, the religions, the two shipwreck stories in parallel, one marvelous, one leaden, the idea of the "better story," and, therefore, of a lesser story, and the choice therein, and how that applied to faith, all of it—tumbled into my mind. It was extraordinarily exciting. After that came about two years or so of research on animals, zoos, religions, and shipwrecks, which inspired me further, and then all the hard, blessed work inherent in writing a novel. It took me four and a half years in all.

Q: This interview will appear in an issue of *Rush Hour* that will have as its theme "Reckless." Is that a word that can be applied to any of your characters or, perhaps, to yourself?

A: It certainly doesn't apply to any of the animals in *Life of Pi*. Animals are never reckless; they're too aware of the dangers lurking about them, and possessed with the fear inherent in that knowledge, to be reckless. And I don't think it applies particularly well to Pi, either. It was nature that was reckless with him, what with its sinking the ship he and his family were on and throwing him in a lifeboat with a tiger.

But I think the word "reckless" might apply to me as a writer, indeed, to all writers and artists. You spend years on a project, you invest yourself completely in it, heart and soul, and nine times out of ten the impact on your times is next to nil. A few good reviews, negligible sales, then silence. And it's fine to be in your twenties and poor and living your dreams, it's fine to be in your thirties and poor and living your dreams—but in your forties it starts to suck to be poor. The specter of failure, that you've thrown away your life for nothing, starts to loom, and it's terrifying. Your dreams haven't paid off, and what are you left with? If *Life of Pi* hadn't connected with readers, I would have been a forty-year-old writer with a skeptical publisher and the CV of a teenager. At best, I could have put under hobbies "writing." The last time I held down a job, I was a security guard and I was in my twenties. With those kinds of professional skills, I might as well have spent those twenty years of writing in jail.

So that's reckless: sitting down and writing a novel.

Q: Why did you choose to interject yourself into the story in a prefatory author's note and italicized interjections throughout the text?

A: One of the first things you have to establish when telling a story is the point of view. Usually it's a choice between first-person narration and third-person. Each has its advantages and disadvantages. First person has immediacy but lacks perspective—you're trapped in the I-voice. Third person has breadth—you can drop into the mind of any character you want—but it can lack intimacy. I chose first person very quickly. The story would be more powerful if the reader was *in* the lifeboat with Pi, hearing him in an unmediated way, not hovering in the air above him. But I also needed to have an outside look at him, how he fared after his tragedy, how he was in Toronto. I needed a frame.

The author's note and the chapters in italics—which, by the way, are short and are only in parts one and three—are that frame, that outside look at the I-voice. In a way, I wanted the best of both worlds, I wanted both first-person and third-person narration.

Q: I have read that a great deal of careful planning went into the writing of the novel. Did the process ever visit surprises on you, nevertheless? Also, why is the story told, as Pi puts it, "in exactly one hundred chapters, not one more, not one less"?

A: Yes, I plan what I write carefully. I couldn't imagine starting a story without knowing exactly where it was going. For me, to do otherwise would be like being an architect asked to start the drawings for a building without being told what the building was for, whether a school or a hospital or a sports center. It's not only that form must follow function, that the shape your story takes must serve its purpose, so that tone and character, for example, will be different depending on whether a story is broadly comedic or dramatic. It's more than that; it's that what comes early in a story surely must have some bearing on what comes later. How can a writer lay down the symbols, the leitmotifs, the hints, the allusions in a story if he or she doesn't know where that story is going? How can you reap if you don't know what you've sown? So two images: the architect and the farmer. Both demand that their work be planned and researched. But that doesn't mean the subsequent work isn't a romp. It was a pleasure doing the research for *Life of*

Pi, on religions, on animal behavior, on zoo biology, on shipwrecks, and it was an equal pleasure weaving all those researched elements together to give full life to the story.

As for the story being told in one hundred chapters, the answer to that is in the novel, in something Pi says at the end of part two, when the tiger abandons him on the beach. Pi emphasizes the importance of doing things well, of good form. He laments the botched goodbye with the tiger. So he feels that a novel in one hundred chapters is also in good form. And I agree. Art is the imposition of order on nature, of form and meaning on what might otherwise have neither. So a novel told in 100 chapters is more pleasing, I think, than one told in, say, 98 chapters. This slanders the number 98, of course. I'm sure a mathematician will find beauty in the number 98. But for the nonmathematician, the number 100 is somehow meaningful and pleasing and the number 98 is arbitrary and unpleasing.

Q: Despite its increasingly magical elements, the story is a marvel of verisimilitude. What kind of research went into its writing?

A: A fair bit. But can one ever know enough about religions and animals? Gods and animals stand at opposite extreme ends of our own, *human* being. With one we reach very high, toward the frame of being, stretching to the limits of our understanding, and with the other we have our original, primal nature, what we once were. We lie somewhere between the two. I could have spent ten years doing research on Christianity, Islam, and Hinduism. Religion fully plumbs the depths of what it means to be human. It and art are the only human endeavors truly worth the effort. And I also loved doing research on shipwrecks and castaways. Nothing like a good story to stir one up, and castaway stories are always amazing. They show life reduced to its simplest, most essential elements, like religion, in a way.

Q: *Life of Pi* has been described as both a fable and an allegory. Is it either and, if not, how would you describe it?

A: The word "story" is good enough for me. How readers take *Life of Pi*, how they interpret it, how they label it, is their business, not mine.

Q: One reviewer has referred to your didactic agenda. Did you have such an agenda?

A: No. A number of topics motivated me in writing *Life of Pi*—principally faith, religion, and storytelling, and in an incidental way animal behavior and zoo biology—but I had no agenda if by agenda you mean a particular intent. A novel should be as rich as a forest. I had as much of an agenda as a forest has.

Q: You have said you grew up in a secular household but *Life of Pi* is clearly a novel about faith. Indeed, one character says the story will make you believe in God. How

did you come to write a book about faith? And would you make a distinction between religion and faith and, for that matter, belief?

A: Yes, the novel is about faith, specifically religious faith, but its argument could apply to any faith—romantic, political, what have you. I argue in the novel that reality—the manner in which we live with it, make our peace with it—is an interpretation, a choice, a selection of elements which determines our reading of it. That being so, I argue for the "better story." I argue that if you have a choice between two interpretations of a given situation—neither of which is delusional, mind you—then why not choose the better story? Why choose less than more? Why not believe that somehow, in a way we can't fully understand, everything about us makes sense? The novel is a kind of gentler Pascal's Wager.

Religion is the usual expression of faith in the divine, or was for the longest time. Nowadays, many people have doubts about organized religion. I have no comment on that. To each his or her own way of understanding what life is about, whether in the traditional way of a Roman Catholic, an orthodox Jew, or an animist, or in a more personal, idiosyncratic way, or in a way that is completely materialist. Each of us must come to some understanding of what it's all about. My only reserve with highly individual, self-determined, "New Age" readings of ultimate reality is that they tend to be self-indulgent and lacking in rigor. As for materialist readings of reality, they're doable, for sure. Entire systems of thinking are based on materialism, Marxist-Leninism being the most obvious example, and most of us in the West today are both stimulated and anesthetized by the relentless materialism of consumerism. But to see only chance chemistry in everything about us, to see only deterministic impulses behind every act of every animate being, is a flat and gray reading.

As for faith and belief, the latter is weaker than the former. Faith leaps where belief remains crouched in doubt. Belief is a reasonable term. I believe in gravity, I believe in the law, I believe in this or that candidate, based on a rational assessment of things.

Faith goes beyond that. It certainly uses reason, but as a means, not as an end. Another way of seeing it is this: Those who believe *cling,* while those who have faith *let go.*

I came to be interested in these questions of faith and religion because they were entirely absent in my youth and I felt something was lacking. I had already made the unreasonable step of becoming a writer; I went one step further in taking on even bigger fictions. The fact is, we're not driven or determined by facts. Facts are the ground upon which we build the fictions that are who we are. Life is not fully knowable through reason. Other tools work fine too: Our emotions are a good one. So is imagination and intuition. In writing *Life of Pi,* I opened myself up to a greater reading of life.

Q: Pi describes reason as "fool's gold for the bright" and perhaps plaintively asks, "Why can't reason give greater

answers?" Do you share his opinions? And, in this context, which is greater: fear or faith? (I'm thinking here of chapter 56.)

A: We're fascinated by reason in the West—and with good reason. The dogged use of reason has resulted in the advances of science and technology, which have transformed not only our lives but the very perception we have of ourselves. But reason is a means, not an end. Reason is good for problem solving. But love and loss, ageing, desire and temptation, ambition and failure, beauty and deception—all these things, they're not *problems*, they're life itself. Who in their right mind, if they were seventy years old and lying in a hospital bed dying of cancer, would say, "I've led a good life, I've been reasonable my whole life?" Reason is only useful if it is put at the service of some faith, whether in God, a political system, art, or your sweetheart. But to be reasonable for its own sake is a waste of life. Life's too short to be entirely reasonable about it.

As for which is the greater of fear and faith, it depends on the situation, doesn't it? One would hope that faith always dominates, but life can be hard and some faiths are misplaced.

Q: Near the end of the book, Pi offers an alternative version of what has happened to him. Is that related to this consideration of reason and faith?

A: Absolutely. It's the heart of the novel. Pi offers two stories to the investigators, one more plausible, one less plausible. He asks them which they believe. They choose the story with animals. Pi replies, "And so it goes with God." Indeed, so it goes with God: The divine—in whatever way you care to consider it—is the better story. Is it *true*? I don't know, and I don't know who in this world could know, just as the investigators can never know what happened to Pi in the Pacific. It's all a matter of faith, faith given vigor and rigor by reason.

Q: Pi says, "I have heard nearly as much nonsense about zoos as I have about God and religion." How are the three related?

A: They're not, except metaphorically perhaps. Some people see zoos as jails for unhappy animals who yearn to be free, while others see religions as jails for unhappy people who yearn to be free. Now, I don't deny that there are zoos and places of worship that are like jails to their inmates. But they're not all like that. The man or woman of true faith is most definitely free, and the fundamental emotion of true religion is joy; you read that in the mystical writings of all faiths, you see it in the eyes of those who have real faith. That's why fundamentalists are so angry, by the way. Because they can't access that joy. So they cling to their narrow beliefs and get endlessly upset, like a frantic animal in a cage that's too small. But the animal in the good zoo lies quietly at rest, content—"free" if you want—within the limits that life, or, in this case, the perceptive and caring zookeeper, has set, just as the person of true faith accepts with joy the limitations that a higher zookeeper has set.

Q: You have said, "Art should be ambitious." Can you expand on that? What are you working on now? And is it more ambitious than *Pi*?

A: I was speaking of my own efforts when I said that. My talent is limited, my time is limited, so I'd rather expend my creative energies on projects that truly matter to me, that say, *Here, this is what I have understood life to be.* Doesn't every writer aspire to significance? That I may fail is beside the point; it's the intent that counts. My next project is a novel on the Holocaust, or, rather, the significance of the Holocaust. My artistic thesis is that we learn from historical events only if they live in our imagination, if they are stories and metaphors that can be retold and applied to new situations, and that one of the reasons we haven't learned all we should from the Holocaust is that we are leery of grappling with it with our imagination. It was such an awful, unprecedented event, so unlike anything humanity had known, that most of us, writers and artists included, are dumbfounded into silence. The result is that most writings on the Holocaust have been of a documentary, literal nature. Think of *The Diary of Anne Frank,* of the writings of Elie Wiesel, Primo Levi, Imre Kertesz, Victor Klemperer. Wiesel once said (I'm paraphrasing him here), "A novel about Auschwitz is either not a novel or not about Auschwitz." Well, that's a serious problem, because our past only lives through the art that it becomes. What is left of Troy but Homer? What is left of Elizabethan England but Shakespeare? I know there are the historical tomes, but those lie within the domain of specialists, of academics. And of course we need those testimonies of Levi and company, and the commentary of academics and historians as well; we need to know the facts, what happened, before we can grapple with them. But ultimately, it's stories that we need. And that's what I'm trying to do, write a properly imaginative novel about the Holocaust, a distillation of it, if you want. If you can't see what that will mean concretely, on the page, don't worry: At the moment, I can't either. The truth is, the Holocaust, like rape, doesn't make for good art. The characters are unlikely and they don't develop. The Nazis are evil from start to finish, without modulation, and the Jews and other victims are forever innocent. Still, I'm going to try. Didn't I say art should be ambitious?

Q: Do you write every day? And are you one of those writers who can write anywhere?

A: I write very little. I mostly think, and then, once something has crystallized in my mind, I write. When I'm in the writing phase of a novel, yes, I can write every day, all day, albeit very slowly, inefficiently, writing two sentences, crossing one out and then taking a break. But when I'm mulling things over, I don't write for weeks and months, except for the odd little jotting.

Q: You have lived in a surprising number of places over the course of your life. How has that influenced you as a writer? Do you regard yourself as a Canadian, or perhaps

I should ask if you regard yourself as a Canadian writer and, if so, what that means to you?

A: Of course I'm a Canadian writer. What else could I be? My residencies and travels abroad as a child and as an adult opened my mind, enriched me, taught me the incredibly varied ways in which we human beings can *be*. The world is a big, beautiful, intoxicating, unsettling place. But everyone has to be from somewhere. There is no international culture or citizenry. I am from Canada, and I'm glad about that. This is a good country: peaceful, tolerant, multicultural, with a fair social policy that seeks the greater good for the greatest number. And across the board, at the federal, provincial, and municipal levels, there's good government support for the arts.

Q: How has winning the Booker Prize changed your life? And has the winning of it made the writing of your next book more or less difficult?

A: The Booker has made my life busier and more complicated, offering me many opportunities and distractions. It's made the writing of my next book more difficult only in that it's been hard finding time. Only now, nearly two and a half years after the Booker, am I finally getting back to writing. But it's changed nothing on the inside. The challenge of writing the next book remains the same: Can I do it? Do I know what I'm doing? Do I know how to do it?

Q: Are literary prizes important?

A: To the extent that they bring attention to books, yes, they are important. Many more people heard of my books thanks to the Booker Prize. It brought me a far greater number of readers than any publicist could have managed. And prizes also make your mother proud, that's another good thing about them.

Q: Your book has attracted a wide readership among teenagers. In fact, Harcourt has published a young adult edition of it. Does that surprise you?

A: Yes. I wrote *Life of Pi* with adults in mind. It's an adult novel, that is, serious and unrestricted. I never wrote it with teenagers in mind. But I'm delighted that they've taken to it. My only fear is that their reading of it will be flattened by pat interpretations of it, that teenagers will not read it with the depth with which an adult might and will never reread it. The sort of fate that has befallen *Lord of the Flies,* say, or *The Old Man and the Sea.*

Q: Have you had much feedback from younger readers?

A: Yes, I've received many letters from young readers. Some are amusing, some are touching, some are homework.

Q: Do you write with an audience in mind?

A: No. Just someone who is intelligent and curious.

Q: What important question have I failed to ask?

A: The question, "What do you think of author interviews?" I'm wary of them, for two reasons: First, if the author is talking about his or her work, because the author is supposed to have greater authority of interpretation (rather than authority of intent), the author's take is held to be "the truth" about the work, which cramps the reader's freedom of interpretation. A book is a meeting between two minds, the writer's and the reader's; I think that meeting should be as free as possible. Second, if the author is *not* talking about his or her work, why bother? Why should the author's opinion be any more interesting or worthy of greater attention than that of any other citizen?

The Braid

Helen Frost

Failte

The Braid begins in 1850, near the end of the Highland Clearances, when thousands of people were evicted from the Western Isles of Scotland (also called the Outer Hebrides). The people had lived on the land for many generations, working hard and paying rent, but when it became more profitable for landlords to raise sheep on the land than to collect rent from their tenants, many of the landlords forced the tenants to leave. Some evicted tenants went to cities in mainland Scotland, some went to America, some to New Zealand and Australia; many went to Canada. They were not rich people, and often they did not have time to pack for the journey. Some left home with little more than the clothes they were wearing.

Around that time, the potato crop failed in many places, including both the Isle of Barra, in Scotland, and Cape Breton, in Canada. This caused widespread hunger among people who depended on potatoes for a large portion of their food. The effect was not so severe on the smaller island of Mingulay, to the south of Barra, in part because people there had a more varied diet, including thousands of seabirds that nested on the island's cliffs.

Failte *means "welcome" in Gaelic, the language spoken in the time and place of the family you are about to meet.*

The Mussel Bailiff

SARAH
Isle of Barra, Scotland, 1850

All of us! Father, Mother, Jeannie, and the wee ones—Willie,
Margaret, and Flora—Grandma Peggy, and myself. We're all
to be evicted come next Monday. Our crime? Nothing more than
hunger: I went with Mother when the tide was out, to gather
mussels for our supper. We filled our basket. Mother strapped it
to her back. We could hear, from down the glen, Old Donald
      playing
on his pipes, a cheerful tune that Mother hummed as we walked
      home.
I was happy. We'd have more than seaweed in our soup that night.
Then comes the mussel bailiff, all high and mighty, like he thinks
he is the Duke himself! Him and his dogs, all snarling at us—
and he takes his knife and cuts the straps from Mother's basket, so
it falls from her shoulders to the mud. He grinds all our mussels
underfoot until the shells are just blue specks, then tells us we're

to leave our home before this week is out. Mussels in that bay,
we're told, are bait for English fishermen, not food for Scottish
children like ourselves. If they let one family take supper
from the bay, soon everyone, they say, will be taking all the
mussels they can eat. *And what,* I think, *would be so wrong with
        that?*
But I know better than to speak such thoughts. I hold my tongue.
The ship is sitting in Lochboisdale, due to sail next Tuesday
if the weather holds. Mother's baking bannocks for our journey;
Father's gone to try to sell his tools, hoping only that they'll
bring enough to pay our passage. It troubles me: how will we
build a house in Canada without them? A table. Benches.
Willie's cradle. Grandma's loom. A new bed for me and Jeannie.
I sit outside with Grandma, knitting. We're trying to be good.
Grandma frowns and clicks her needles like she's telling them
the thoughts she tries to silence. She's in no mood for talking. But
I have so many questions. The day we'll leave is coming close.
Who else can I ask? I lean on Grandma's shoulder: *How long will
the journey be? How big is the ship? Will there be dogs and cats
in Canada?* As I expect, she shushes me. She says she
has no answers. I grow silent, breathing in the smell of her
wool shawl, the smell of peat smoke and the sea, the sour smell
        where
Willie spat up on her shoulder after breakfast. At last she
speaks: *Child, my heart is breaking, but I'll not be going with you.
I'll take my weaving from the loom and go back to Mingulay
where I was born. My William's buried in the graveyard there, and
some days I expect that I may well be there beside him soon.*

Then she takes my head into her hands and weeps. When she sees
      tears
on my face, she wipes them with her fingers, soft and rough at
      once.
I know she wants to hold me here. I know too that she'll not try.
She gathers up her tangled wool, takes her basket back inside.

The Braid

JEANNIE
Isle of Barra

Willie fussed, and wouldn't go to sleep. It was late, we were
all packed, ready for the journey. Sarah held him tighter
than she usually does. She looked long at his face and then she
gathered him up, kissed his nose, wrapped her shawl around him,
      pulled
it—pulled Willie—close. She looked at Flora, then at Margaret,
playing on the floor with the wee rag doll we made for her.
Home. Sarah must have thought. *Remember this.* Later that same
night—we could not sleep—we walked together to the cove.
      Father
thinks that Sarah must have told me then. She did not. None of
us—not even I—knew what she was planning. Sarah was
so quiet. She didn't laugh when an otter opened a
mussel with a rock and ate it, and I made my wee joke:
We'll tell the bailiff—you'll be sent to Canada with us. The
bay was still. Moonlight on the water made a path from our

Scottish sea to—where? Where, I wonder, will we all be eating
supper in two months' time? One year? I linked arms with Sarah,
the way we've done since we were small, sitting and watching on
that rock. Then we dipped our hands into the sea and touched our
tongues to the seawater, each of us swallowing a bit.
Tuesday still seemed far off then, the salty sea so close, our
journey not yet started. We walked back home. *Hush now,* Sarah
        said,
they'll be asleep. So they were, but we were wide awake when
we went to our bed. I took the hairbrush from the wooden
bench, and sat by Sarah, brushing out her long thick hair. *Oh.*
Jeannie . . . Sarah whispered. *I can't . . .* She drew in her breath.
        Then . . .
Goodnight. (Or did she say *goodbye*?) She loosened my braids,
        held
them in her hand and brushed my hair so hard—I should have
        known.
But how could I? Then Sarah braided my hair with her own,
close and tight, so our heads were touching. We started laughing.
Will you girls go to sleep? It's near morning! Father called. Like two
cats curled together, we slept that night. Or—did Sarah sleep?
She must have stayed awake until I slept. She must have had
her sewing scissors tucked into her pocket. Sarah knew
where she was going. I woke to no warm place beside me.
She'd cut the braid close to our heads, tucked half into my hand—
        You / me / sisters / always.
Now we're in the boat, and leaving;

Mingulay is but a distant blur. We've left without her—
and I want to dive into the sea and swim back home. But
soon we will be out too far to see the hills where Sarah's
tears are no doubt falling like my own. I squeeze my right hand
once, around the braid in my pocket. Father says, *Be strong.*
Try to be as helpful as you can. Your mother needs you.
Inside, I'm still crying. *I'll hold Margaret's hand,* I say.

After Three Days

SARAH
Isle of Barra

Were they angry? Could they understand how this place holds
      me, so
tight I could not live away from it? Nor could I leave Grandma.
She scolded, but she was pleased, when, after three days, my
      hunger
pulled me back here. That first day, I hid and watched their boat go
      out—
Margaret kneeling at the bow, arms spread like a bird. Behind
her, Mother, strong and watchful, one hand upon her shoulder, the
same way she watched me when I was four. Flora sat straight
      beside
Father. Jeannie held Willie. No doubt she sang to him. Boxes
of food for the journey, and two other men—the fishing boat
was full. A man named Ranald took them to Lochboisdale. He has

a younger brother going to Canada by choice. Jeannie
joked: *He should go in place of one of us*—perhaps now she
          thinks
the joke has turned out true.
Grandma tells me about Mingulay:
Our life will not be easy. We'll have fish and birds and eggs to
eat; I have no fear of starving. But winters can be long—and,
Sarah, only twenty families live there. You'll be lonesome
on your own. She looks hard at me. *I'll have you,* I say. She blinks.
Our journey there is likely to be rough. Some say it's every
bit as daunting as the trip to Canada....Well, then. We link
our arms and walk down to the cove. *Sarah's coming, too,*
          Grandma
says to Murdo Campbell, the young fisherman who's taking us.
When he sees me, arm in arm with Grandma Peggy, clenching my
wooden walking stick like it's my sister, I can't guess his thoughts.
Oh, Sarah, don't you worry, now, Grandma Peggy says (I know
then, I should be worried). *If anyone can land a boat or*
hold us steady in a stormy sea, it's Murdo Campbell. He's
known for landing safely on Mingulay when others can't. My
own thoughts I keep to myself: Have I been foolish? Is this man
laughing at me? I know my hair must look odd where I cut it;
two patches on my skirt are coming loose; the past three nights I've
slept out in the hills, with little food. *Here,* Murdo says, *I*
had two old waterproofs at home, and brought them both. You'd
          think I
knew that you were coming, Sarah. I take the small one. He looks
me up and down—as if he's weighing me—then shifts his anchor,

hands me a bailer—*just in case*—seats Grandma Peggy to his
left, me to his right, and pushes us out to sea. Grandma folds
her hands and bows her head. I look up at Murdo—his eyes calm,
but merry, arms pulling hard on the oars. He looks at me. *Aye.*
Sarah, they'll be glad, on Mingulay, to have a lively lass.
Hand me that parcel, would you? He opens it and offers me
strong tea, still hot, and a hard-boiled egg. *The birds are calling to*
you, he says, pointing overhead: gulls circling, screeching. If they
say anything, it's likely, *You, there—where do you think you're going?*

Chain of Events

Elizabeth E. Wein

Mom and I are dozing off our jet lag on the hotel terrace when the red-and-blue seaplane arrives. We watch it circle Loch Craigie three times before it comes diving in to settle on the water's surface. It floats down almost soundlessly, and so steeply that at first I think it's in trouble and is going to crash. But then the bright little plane is taxiing, obviously with precision and expertise, on the water in the middle of the loch.

It slows down as it comes to the boat dock. A boy about my own age gets out first, jumping onto one of the plane's floats. His father hands him a couple of small tires, and the boy wedges them beneath the floats as the plane glides onto the stony beach.

"Look at that, Evie. That's the way to travel," my mother says admiringly.

"Show-offs," I say.

We're both envious. My mother is the kind of person who can't sit still for more than five minutes at a time. If there's something to be done, she does it. She's tired now, but she'd still rather be mooring a seaplane than taking a nap in the sun. She envies the action. I do too, but in a different way. I envy the initiative. My mother makes me lazy. It's much easier to go along with her obviously good ideas than to come up with my own.

I'm like this with my friends, too. Even when I get an idea about what we should do, I let other people organize it. It bothers me, sometimes; it's like a bad habit that I can't seem to break—just going with the flow. I tell myself I shouldn't let it bother me if I'm enjoying myself anyway. But it does.

This vacation in Scotland, for example, is my mother's idea. It's my high school graduation present, a mother-and-daughter trip together. We're staying in the Grampian Mountains. Our hotel is about a hundred and fifty years old, but it looks like a medieval castle. There's a real castle, smaller and ruined, on an island in the middle of the loch. There's a nine-hole golf course, and fishing boats, and you have to *dress for dinner*. When the boy from the plane comes into the dining room for the first time, they won't let him in until he goes away and puts on a tie.

I think he is delicious. He is black-haired and slender, and offhandedly funny. His name is Connell. His dad is straightforward and generous, buying drinks for everybody in the bar after dinner. They're from northern England; they live in the Lake District and have come to Scotland for a vacation, like us. My mother the organizer strikes a bargain with Connell's father. She's going to take him in her rented car to spend a day playing golf at St. Andrew's while she shops for souvenirs, and he'll take her flying in his seaplane.

I'm half-pleased, half-annoyed with her for striking this deal. How can a forty-two-year-old woman be so bold? And she always just assumes I'll go along with any plan she makes. At least it means a couple of hours in the car with Connell. I'll be forced to talk to him, squashed together in the backseat of our tiny rental.

But Connell is not as easily led as I am. He takes one look at the car the next morning and refuses to get in.

"Forget it," he says. "Not enough leg room. I don't mind staying here; I'll hike up Mount Craigie. I'm not much of a golfer."

My mother opens her mouth and shuts it again, probably deciding against trying to tempt him with the allure of Kingdom of Fife Cashmere.

But I'm disappointed, and I make a simple move that is really a small act of rebellion.

"I'll climb Mount Craigie with you."

My mother stares at me, then grins. She's probably been waiting for this moment all her life. "Are you sure, Eve?"

"If it's okay," I add hastily, feeling myself going red in the face.

"It's fine," says Connell.

So the adults fold themselves into the toy car and leave us standing in fitful sun and shadow on the gravel apron in front of the hotel. Connell glances sideways at me from beneath the black hair, with a kind of impish, hopeful expression that makes him look about ten.

"Now we're going to *have* to talk to each other," he says.

I laugh, because that's exactly what I'm thinking.

"Don't worry," I say. "I've got lots of questions."

The obvious one spills out before I can stop myself. But I have to ask, because I think it's so damn cool: "Is that your dad's plane?"

"We're in a syndicate. Four of us own it together. One of them didn't pass his medical this year and the other one lives in London, so Dad and I get the most use out of it."

"Can *you* fly?" I ask, in awe.

"Of course," Connell answers carelessly, tossing the hair from his eyes. Then he adds, "I'll take you up, if you want."

"Really? Just like that? Where can we go?"

"Anywhere. We can fly to the next loch and have a picnic."

"What a great idea!"

I run back to the room I share with my mother and scrounge through our collection of travel essentials. I put together a motley picnic in a shopping bag and look around the room, wondering what else I might need for a joyride in a seaplane. Connell was wearing rubber boots when he landed, I remember. Your feet get wet, getting in and out.

Here I am again, going along with someone else's great idea.

Yes, so? What's wrong with that? I kick off my sneakers and dig a pair of flip-flops out of my suitcase. And my beach towel, and a folding poncho made out of thin plastic

like a big garbage bag, emblazoned PHILADELPHIA HIGH
SCHOOL FOR GIRLS. We can sit on that if the ground is
wet. And my camera.

Connell's banging on the door. I grab my shopping bag
and join him in the hall. He's got a laminated map tucked
under his arm.

"You'll have to help me get the plane out on the water,"
he says. "You have to pass me the tires so we can moor
somewhere else if we want to."

We sling the food and the tires and the mooring rope
into a little well in the back of the plane. It is tiny, absolutely tiny, inside. The two seats are one behind the
other.

"God, it's smaller than the car!" I say. "A flying bicycle!"

"Please. A flying pedal boat!" Connell answers.

We both laugh. I like his sense of humor.

"You get in the back," he directs me. "You can wear my
headset. I'll wear Dad's. We don't need to talk to anybody
on the radio. We won't go anywhere near controlled air-
space, but we can talk to each other."

"Okay."

We strap ourselves in, Connell ahead of me. He doesn't
explain much about what's going on; he concentrates on
getting the plane going. I can tell it's old; there's no ignition
key. Connell pushes a little button on the dashboard to
start the engine. It's so crazy: This airplane just sits on the
water where anyone could climb in and start it up and fly
off with it. It occurs to me that Connell's father doesn't
know we're doing this. But Connell seems so confident and
in control; surely he wouldn't be flying his father's plane if

he wasn't allowed to. And it's not my problem if he gets in trouble.

We skate over the loch with the power way up.

"It's a flying Jet Ski!" I yell. Connell is still concentrating and doesn't answer. His left hand is constantly fooling with levers in the wall of the plane. The thing on the window that looks like a latch is actually the throttle—I can tell by the change in the sound of the engine when Connell fiddles with it.

Then suddenly the plane seems to come unstuck, like a suction cup unsealing itself from the surface of the water, and we aren't coasting anymore; we're soaring.

The sides of the glen rise steeply beneath us. It takes time for the plane to labor to the height of the hill, and although Loch Craigie is now a couple of hundred feet below us and steadily falling farther away, the hillside isn't any more than fifty yards out the window.

"See the deer?" Connell asks abruptly, pointing.

I uncurl my fingers from the edge of my seat and look out at the mountainside. There's a herd of about fifty red deer, racing below us over invisible footholds along the nearly sheer hillside. I'm too slow to get a picture of them, but I take a couple of shots of the mountains wreathed so dramatically in cloud.

We travel along another glen, at a level with the barren hill crests.

"Why don't you go higher?" I ask. "We seem so close to the ground."

"We're at two and a half thousand feet; that's safe. The cloud's too low for us to climb much higher. We don't want to end up in a cloud! I'm not instrument rated; I can only fly if I can see."

The way between the hills is clear enough. The green valley below us is utterly empty. There's not even a track or a wall; it feels like we're the first people ever to see this landscape.

"There's the next loch," says Connell, pointing ahead; and as he does it, the engine coughs and goes silent.

I'm glad I'm behind him and can't see the expression on his face. I see that casual hand on the windowsill go rigid. He jerks on the knob I've worked out is the throttle, then pumps it desperately; when nothing happens there, he pushes and pulls another button in the side of the door. The plane is gently gliding lower, but not plummeting out of the sky, and I don't know if I should be panicking or not. I pray for the engine to start, but nothing happens.

"I'll have to land in the valley," Connell says in an incredibly steady voice. He sounds calm but strangled.

"Can you do that on floats?"

"I can't take off again if I do. The engine's failed, but don't worry, I can land."

"Are we out of gas?" I ask.

"Gas?" he croaks.

They use something else in Scotland, or call it something else. Petrol? Not in planes—"Fuel. Are we out of fuel?"

"Fuel!"

Connell shouts it. His hand flies to another lever, and flips it over. He works at the throttle again, and the engine fires happily back to life.

"Fuel! Thank you *God*," Connell says unnecessarily.

"You can call me Eve," I answer.

Connell chokes with laughter. The aircraft is climbing now. I keep my mouth shut as we gain height. It's too easy to make him laugh. I don't want to distract him.

"What happened there?" I ask, feeling extremely pleased with myself for not having panicked.

"I forgot to switch fuel tanks. There's one in each wing. When one's empty the feed doesn't automatically switch to the other; you have to do it manually . . ."

He clears his throat.

"Dad usually leaves them pretty full, to keep down the condensation, but I guess he hasn't filled them. Oh—" Now the plane is flying level with the cloud-strewn mountaintops again. "I *know* he hasn't filled them, because he asked your mother to stop at the airport in Dundee so he could get them to send up a bowser for him. He thought he would have better luck in person than over the phone. So that means—"

"—there isn't much fuel in the other tank?"

"I don't know," Connell says in a sepulchral voice, trying to be funny and make light of it. He banks the plane in what I think must be a dangerously tight turn. I sit on my hands so that I won't do something silly like grip the back of Connell's seat, or worse, his shoulders. Or worse, hit him in the head.

"I don't know," Connell says again, but speaking normally this time. "I didn't check the fuel level. Anyway, I think we should turn back."

He has already made the turn. The engine putters

reliably. The cloud forces us lower and lower, but I know that the open water of Loch Craigie is waiting for us at the end of the glen.

Only, by the time we reach the loch, the clouds have closed above us and a blanket of fog at least fifty feet thick covers everything below us.

It's amazing. The black keep of ruined Craigie Castle juts above the sea of white fog like a scene in a fairy tale. If I look south, toward where the hotel is supposed to be, I can see a line of blue sky between the endless gray cloud above and the endless white fog below. That's the direction of St. Andrews, so the sun is shining on our parents.

Connell makes the plane circle in the mouth of the valley.

"You can't land now, can you?" I ask. "Or whatever you call it." Do you "land" on water?

He doesn't answer. We continue to circle, which I find very disorienting. I look for the green valley we came down, but all I can see is fog.

Then we're flying in a straight line again, but there's fog below us as well as cloud above. We can see the steep mountain slopes on either side of us, but not the ground.

"We're in a sandwich," I say.

"Be quiet a minute," Connell says. "I'm going to make a radio call. Don't say anything while they're talking to me."

I shut up. Connell launches into conversation with someone he calls "Scottish Information." I have trouble following this because the air traffic language seems so coded. They're talking about the weather, and fog. Connell tells them he's low on fuel. He also says he's going to try the next loch again.

"Stay on frequency," I hear them tell him, and then there is silence for such a long time, as we make our way yet again up the valley *away* from Loch Craigie, that I finally ask, "What's pan pan pan?"

"It's 'pan pan.' You say 'pan pan' three times. It's an urgency call, not an emergency. It's *like* an emergency, except your plane isn't in immediate danger."

"Oh."

I'm quiet again, and then say with deeply false cheer, "Well, at least we're not lost."

Connell does not answer. Every now and then you can see a thread of green below us.

The valley opens up over the place where the next loch is supposed to be. It's another cotton-filled trough of blind fog.

"You said you could land in the valley, when the engine stopped," I say. "But you can't see well enough to land there now, can you?"

"No."

"And you really don't have any idea how much fuel we've got?"

"Please be still," he hisses. It's a firm command, a pilot's command. He's in control, and he's trying to decide what to do.

If the engine stops now, he can't see where to land. And he hasn't got another fuel tank to switch to.

Then I begin to feel sick. How did we get here? We were

irresponsible, okay, we didn't get permission to go, we didn't tell anyone where we were going. And careless, okay, we were careless, we didn't check the fuel supply or the weather. But we hadn't been *crazy:* We didn't set out to do anything daredevil or dangerous; we knew where our limits were, we hadn't tried anything we couldn't do. How did we get here, half a mile above the ground with no way to get back to it except to hurl ourselves at it blindly and hope we don't get crushed or drown in the impact?

"There's another loch on the other side of that hill straight ahead of us," Connell says quietly, looking at his map. "It's higher up than this one, and maybe it'll be clear."

We'll just about make it over the top of the ridge ahead, scraping through a gap between the ground and the cloud. Our choice is to try that, or wait for the fuel to run out and force us out of the sky. It isn't a choice.

"Okay," I say.

Connell repeats this plan to the blind authorities, who wait helplessly in a radio station somewhere miles away, wondering what's happening to us.

We chug on over the top. I look down. Dark water lies plainly visible not much more than three or four hundred feet below us. The mountain pool is perfectly round, like a little black eye surrounded by walls of rock; from where we are it doesn't look much bigger than a fishpond. It's a very sinister, barren landscape too, but I think I've never seen anyplace so beautiful.

Connell makes another radio call to say we're going to land.

"Roger," crackles the disembodied voice, and that's the

last we hear from them, because once we're down below the rim of the bowl made by the mountains we lose contact with them.

We make the same steep gliding plummet that Mom and I watched from the hotel terrace yesterday. We touch the water smoothly, and Connell cuts the power to practically nothing. We putter up, can you believe it, to a tiny beach of white sand at one end of the black pool, like the eyelid of the mountain's staring eye.

Then we both sit there, breathing very quietly. God, the *relief.* It seems astonishing to be on the ground again.

"What do we do now?" I say.

"Have our picnic?"

His voice is a little unsteady. But he's trying to be funny again, which I guess is a good sign.

We get out of the plane and pull it a little ashore. There are tufts of bracken growing among the quartz at the foot of the mountain slope, but no grass, no trees, nothing that doesn't seem to be able to cling to sheer rock.

The first thing Connell does is check the fuel.

"It's not too bad," he says. "We could get back. Let's eat lunch, and give the fog time to clear."

He gets my plastic bag out of the plane and hands it to me. My appetite disappeared somewhere over the fog and hasn't come back yet. I'm thinking about the takeoff we made earlier, about how much gentler the slope of the climb out was compared to that steep swooping dive to land again.

"There isn't room to take off here, is there?" I ask. "This lake's too short."

"You don't have to climb in a straight line. You can take off in a spiral, in a seaplane." He stands there, considering. "If I can't get on the step—what you called Jet-Skiing—I won't try the takeoff."

And suddenly I realize that I have to fight this. If he does something stupid and I don't try to stop him, I'm as stupid as he is.

"No," I say. "I'm not going back."

"What?" He looks at me in utter disbelief. We stand on the bone-white sand in the middle of utter nowhere and glare at each other.

"*No,*" I say. "No! I won't do it. You wouldn't get in our car, and I'm not getting in your plane."

"It's safe! You won't get hurt! We won't take off if I can't work up enough speed!"

"I'm not *worried* about the takeoff!" I yell. "I'm worried about the next *landing*! How do you know Loch Craigie won't be covered with fog when we get back there for the *second time*? Then we really *will* be out of fuel! Don't you ever think ahead about *anything*?"

He goes white. He turns away from me with a start, as though I've hit him, as though I've slapped him in the face.

"What about the people you talked to on the radio?" I remind him. "They know where we are, don't they? Won't they send out a search party or something? All we have to do is wait, and someone will come and get us out of here safely."

Connell takes a deep breath, like he's embarrassed to be having a fight with his passenger.

"But if we save them the trouble—" he says, almost pleading. "I have to be *responsible*." He's the pilot.

"I'm being responsible for myself," I say stubbornly, "and I'm not getting back in that plane."

He knows I mean it.

"We'll wait till the clouds lift," he says. "How about that? There's a front passing through, they said. It'll clear up later."

So now we're stuck here waiting for the weather to change or for a rescue team to turn up, and we don't know how long either of those will take. We're not in any real danger, we won't die of thirst, and we haven't wrecked the plane. These are all *good* things, right?

Connell sits down on the white sand, leaning back on his elbows with his ankles crossed and his eyes fixed on the gap below the clouds. He looks like a movie star, even sulking in his rubber boots, against this dramatic highland scenery next to the bright little red-and-blue plane. I take a picture of them.

Connell turns his head slowly to look at me.

"I might have to kill you," he says.

"Don't kill me," I say. "You look great."

He shakes his head. I realize something, watching him sitting there silently staring at the horizon. He's not the pilot anymore. He's given me control.

We wait and wait and wait. Our appetites return, and we eat the apples I've brought, and drink the two cans of soda. It starts to rain.

"Welcome to Scotland," says Connell.

We sit in the plane. It seems like we sit there for hours, and still the rain goes on, and now the wind is picking up, too. Gusts lift the wingtips and the cockpit bumps a little, as though there's a cow outside giving the plane gentle nudges. The rain-spattered windows around and above us look like pebbled glass.

Connell says something so quietly I can't hear him.

"What?"

He repeats himself, not much louder. "Chain of events."

"Chain of events?" I ask.

Connell explains in that same sober, quiet voice. He shifts around in the pilot's seat with one arm over the seat back, so he can look at me. His black hair makes his face look very white.

"Accidents aren't caused by one thing only," he says. "Most accidents aren't caused by one big catastrophe. Pilots don't usually have heart attacks in the air. Wings don't suddenly drop off. Most accidents happen because you do a lot of little things wrong."

Like not telling anyone we were going. And not checking the fuel level. Not asking about the weather before we left. All of it together. If we'd done only one of those things we didn't bother with, none of this would have happened.

"The way to avoid the accident is to break the chain," Connell continues. "You have to recognize how the mistakes are piling up. If you can get rid of just one of the links, you can avoid the accident."

"But we did," I say. "We didn't have an accident."

He winces. "Here we are."

"You can have a *good* chain of events, can't you?" I say. "You can do a lot of little things that help it all turn out right. Knowing you're in trouble and not panicking. Remembering to switch fuel tanks. Talking to the people on the radio so someone knows where we are. Not killing me for taking your picture."

Connell says quietly, "You made the right call, Eve. It's a good thing we're not flying in this."

"I'm sorry I was bossy."

"You're not, usually, are you? It doesn't come naturally."

"I wouldn't make a good pilot."

"You don't need to be bossy to fly a plane," Connell says. "You just need to make sensible decisions. And do it quickly. And don't let anyone change your mind. You have control."

We sit for a while longer. Then the wind lifts the wings so high that the floats actually rise off the beach and come down again with a muffled bang. We both yelp in surprise and fright. The wash of relief when the jolt is over makes my knees go watery, like they did once when I was driving my mother's car and narrowly missed running over a kid on a bicycle.

"We'd better tie the plane down," Connell says.

We've brought the ropes with us, but there isn't a single thing to tie them to. The beach is log and rock free, and the ropes don't reach to the mountainside even after we've dragged the plane completely out of the water. We're both soaking wet now, and we have to hang on to the wing struts to keep the plane from lifting off the ground. "Can you fill the floats?" I ask. "You pumped water out of them before we left Loch Craigie. What if we filled them up with water? That would help weigh the plane down."

"That's a good idea, except we won't be able to take off again even if the weather gets better. My father is going to kill me," Connell mutters. He opens the float covers. "But he'll probably do that anyway."

We can't fill the floats with the bilge pump. Connell cuts the tops off our empty soda cans with his pocketknife, and we fill them and his rubber boots with lake water, and form a kind of assembly line. My flip-flops neither hold water nor keep it out. My feet are very cold.

"What time is it?" I ask, when we've finished filling the floats. We still have to sit on them to keep the wings down, but you can tell the plane's not going to go anywhere. We've done a pretty good job.

"Half past five."

"Time for supper," I say.

"What have you got?"

"Pennsylvania Dutch sourdough pretzels and chocolate."

Connell laughs. "What the bloody hell is a sourdough pretzel?"

For about a quarter of an hour we're warm, from all that work, and the chocolate helps. But the wind and rain are relentless. It's pretty obvious no one is going to be able to rescue us until the weather improves. At least it's June, and we've still got about five hours of daylight.

"What if no one gets here till tomorrow?" I say.

"Don't think about it," says Connell.

Our big problem is the wind. If we could only sit in the

plane, we'd be a little drier. After a while we *can't* get warm, no matter how we stamp our legs and stretch our arms. We take turns wrapping ourselves in my beach towel, which is still more or less dry, and my plastic bag poncho. Fifteen minutes each at a time.

The wind dies down before it gets dark.

"What time is it?"

"Half past nine."

"What time does the sun set?"

"Half past ten."

It's gloomy already, though, because of the cloud.

"There's more chocolate," I say.

"We should probably save it."

He doesn't add, in case we're here all night, but I know he's thinking it.

At least we can get up and walk around now, so I do, trying to get warm. It's still drizzling. It's very tempting to climb into the plane and curl up and go to sleep, except we're both so *wet*. And it's not dark yet. There's nothing to do, but it seems like we should be setting up camp or something.

Connell is still sitting on the end of a float, all wrapped up in my Girls' High poncho, his black hair plastered to his head, shivering and miserable. One of his boots is standing next to him, full of water. Very quietly, I go and poke around in the cockpit for my camera again so I can take another picture of him: before and after.

He looks up, but doesn't move. He says, ominously, "That camera is going to end up somewhere the sun doesn't shine."

"Oh, and what do you call this place, the Virgin Islands?"

"The Bermuda Triangle," Connell says.

His lame attempt at humor hits me like a ray of sunlight. I am weak with relief to hear him wisecracking again; I suddenly realize how serious he's been all afternoon.

"The bonny bonny banks of Loch Montego Bay," I say, equally uninspired, but trying valiantly to encourage him.

"Let me take a picture of you," Connell says.

"No, you'll just throw my camera in the Caribbean."

"Do it as an exercise in trust."

"What about—"

Then we hear the sound of a helicopter.

We look up. You can't miss it: It's bright orange. It passes at an angle from left to right across the gap in the hills at the other end of the loch. It seems like they can't possibly miss us, either, with our bright red-and-blue plane on the white sand, but it's getting dark, and we're behind them. If they flew across the rim of our mountain bowl ahead of us, they might not have looked back at this end of the loch.

Connell jumps up. He stands on the beach yelling and waving my towel. We've got nothing else to signal with, no smoke, no fire, no flare.

I take a picture of the helicopter, a ball of light on the horizon in the gathering dark.

"What in hell—?" Connell starts to say to me, but then he realizes what I'm doing, and shuts up. I hold the camera over my head and shoot flash after flash at the departing

helicopter. And they see it. They see it. They turn around and head back for us.

Connell grabs me by the wrist. For a moment I think he's trying to get the camera out of my hand. Then he pulls me close and *kisses me.*

"My God, you'd make a good pilot, Eve," he says.

THE NEW GIRL

by Tommy Kovac

I PLAYED THE PERFECT SON GAME, AND GOT STRAIGHT As. BUT I WAS BURNING OUT, TURNING INWARD.

ONE BLUSTERY DAY IN EARLY OCTOBER I WAS SITTING IN HONORS ENGLISH WHEN THE DOOR BANGED OPEN AND AUTUMN BLEW IN.

SHE WAS NEW.

HERE.

WANT SOME?

IT WAS VODKA.

AUTUMN AND I BECAME BEST FRIENDS.

Little Sisters Steal the Best Shit

Bennett Madison

You take a seashell. You take a tube of lip gloss and a silk scarf. You take a mountain, and a cloud, and a molten pebble from the core. DeeDee said that this was how we were going to do it. Because the entire planet Earth is pretty fucking big. You have to start small and take a chunk at a time.

When I was fourteen years old—a year before my brother died—my friend DeeDee was going to steal everything. And I mean: every single thing. It is easy to be ambitious when you're fourteen, and it's especially easy if you are DeeDee Knight. She saw no reason that she couldn't have it all—and PS, she wanted it for free. To get what she was after, a partner was necessary. DeeDee chose me.

Between the two of us, we could have done it. A piece at a time, a piece at a time. A cashmere sweater, a plastic charm bracelet. You take a ball of lint, and a handful of grass and some twigs. Steal a piece of earth. Make off with the Great Pyramids. DeeDee had no doubt that we could cram the entirety of existence into our little black purses. And no one would notice our game until we were jetting for the last exit. Truly, we were that good. Too bad we never made it past the shopping mall.

The first thing DeeDee ever stole was a tiny red notebook from right next to the cash register at Waldenbooks—with the clerk looking straight at her. In that notebook, she kept an itemized list of everything she took. Open the cover and it read: "1. Tiny Red Notebook." Number one is easy to remember because I was right there when she wrote it. But sometimes I want to know: What is the last thing on DeeDee's list? There always has to be an end, even if you can't imagine it. So what was the official last thing and what does the end look like when captured on paper in pink ballpoint pen? Maybe it just says, THE END.

The beginning is not so hard to pin down. She taught me to shoplift a week or so after Valentine's Day. She had just turned fourteen. That day, we stood together, at the top of the escalator, looking out over the mezzanine. The shiny marble tiles and the glowing fountains were laid out below us like an instruction manual. We had to follow.

At the mall, DeeDee took on the aspect of myth— something Norse, I'd say, because they're the most imposing, not to mention blond. And was she blond. That first day, she was gilded in glass-elevator gold, bracing herself, palms on the railing. From the third level, she leaned out over it all and whispered, "This is our kingdom." Her voice was hoarse from Newports, and it was hard to tell exactly how sarcastic she was being. I remember, at that moment, I saw sparks fly from her hoop earrings and wondered if maybe the girl was made of electricity.

That day, we sat on the bench outside the Limited, on the ground floor of the mall. "There are three and only three tools for shoplifting," she instructed me, her teardrop pendant quivering in the perfect hollow of her neck. "Number one: a shopping bag. From expensive stores is best. Fill it with something like balled-up newspaper. Number two: a rubber band. Keep it wrapped around your wrist and a few extras in your pocket." She licked her lips because she liked them to be always shiny. "Number three is liquid eyeliner. Applied heavily and frequently."

"Why?" I could have asked. *Why a rubber band? What is the reason?* But I didn't bother. Maybe it had to do with DeeDee's eyes, which were green, smoky, and smeared black, black, black. Like Cleopatra or a pro football player. Those eyes made it hard to concentrate. Or. Not the eyes, I guess, but the liner. Liquid. Applied heavily and frequently.

DeeDee wore high heels and a baseball cap. I thought she was beautiful. I thought this because it was completely true.

At Nordstrom in the summer, DeeDee and I held our purses close to our hips and closer to our fingers. She led the way. I will show you how she did it.

DeeDee had her eye on a pair of sunglasses. The bubblehead behind the display was glaring at her, all raised eyebrow and tooth-baring grin, but DeeDee just smiled and smoothed her ponytail. She looked the clerk in the eye and pursed her lips and when I glanced back at the rack, the glasses were gone—if not in DeeDee's back pocket, then somehow in mine. It was always like that. Because she was the best. She had the kind of secret knowledge that only pumps from the sneakiest heart.

Compared to DeeDee, I was a total amateur. I was always fumbling; I didn't have her cool. Maybe DeeDee was so good because she had a mission. She tried to explain it to me once, that summer, when we were lounging on the concrete floor of the parking garage, watching boys fly around on their skateboards.

"We are stealing this stuff because it belongs to us," she told me while they whizzed through the air, pants barely hanging on. DeeDee was puffing self-consciously on a long, skinny Newport. "Do you think we were born to live in this crappy suburb, to hang out all day in this fake-o palace? No way. Think of it all as our inheritance. They're the ones who stole it from us. We just need to take it back."

"You already have an inheritance," I pointed out. "Your mom sits at home on her butt all day ordering Franklin Mint dolls from catalogs while the family money rolls in."

"That's not what I'm talking about," DeeDee told me.

It was the summer. We wore the tallest platform sandals and the shortest skirts. It was all part of DeeDee's strategy. "We will be like the sun," she said. "Too beautiful to look at. We will never be caught."

"My brother is dying," I said. It came out of nowhere. DeeDee furrowed her brow and looked at me with nervous sympathy. She reached behind her own shoulder and tugged at her ponytail.

"Duh," she said softly. "Where have you been?" DeeDee took my hand and squeezed it so hard that I saw her knuckles turn white.

Pretty soon, it was winter.

That winter, the shopping mall light was deep and gold, offering warm protection. In December standing by the cosmetics counter we could hear the pianist playing Christmas carols from a carpeted alcove near the escalators. The winter that my brother died, the mall smelled like newness; like the future. Or maybe I was just mistaking the smell of cinnamon and makeup. In the glass elevator, DeeDee and I both stared through her reflection as the food court receded and the Christmas lights approached. "What is the most beautiful thing?" she wanted to know. "Because we need to find it and take it."

So we searched hard. I followed her lead, flanking her every step. Stealing right while she stole left. We stole Egyptian cotton bedsheets and bottles of perfume and leather handbags and more costume jewelry than one person could wear in a lifetime. Most days, we'd drop in on Liz, who had been my brother's girlfriend before he'd taken up faggotry. Now she was assistant manager at the Gap. Liz would give us the run of the place, distracting the real manager while we dismantled the store, taking one of almost everything, and sometimes two. DeeDee thought it was sort of cheating, because it wasn't really a challenge with Liz's help, but I didn't see the difference, myself. Free was free. And after the Gap, we'd keep on going. Bras and silver-plated pens and Christmas ornaments. DeeDee stole a crystal figurine of a girl riding on a unicorn—for her mother—and at the last minute decided to keep it for herself. We never did find that most beautiful thing.

At the end of each day, or earlier if we were nervous about security, we'd retreat to our headquarters: the handicap stall. The handicap bathroom at any mall is always deserted and is generally hidden somewhere in a dim alcove near Sears or JCPenney. There's usually a ladies room by the food court too, but DeeDee and I tried to avoid those because they were always full of bulimics. The wheelchair stall was important because it was big enough for two people and the door went all the way to the tiles so no one could tell that you were in there. The wheelchair stall was where we took the loot from our bags, unballed it, and held it out at arm's length, admiring it all under spastic white light.

One time DeeDee and I kissed in there. The handicap stall of the ladies room, Montgomery Mall on a Wednesday afternoon. We'd just hit the Express, hit it hard. DeeDee'd stolen a leather skirt the color of the tropics and I'd crammed a silk blouse into the bottom of my purse. Big scores. DeeDee's lips were waxy and kiwi-strawberry and I put my hand on hers, my fingertips smooth against her round and shiny nails. DeeDee, with her usual abandon, slipped me some tongue. That time I kissed DeeDee, fluorescent lights lit us like jellyfish shining miles below everything. All of it to say: We are sisters, we are a deadly man-o'-war.

It was shortly after that that we were caught for the first time. It had been my fault. Maybe it was because I was getting bored with the routine, bored with the uselessness of shiny things that were good for nothing at all. It seemed like the only place to go was bigger. To steal more and more and more, the most expensive junk, in ridiculous quantity. I got carried away.

We were at Sephora when it happened, and I wasn't paying attention to anything at all, not even to what I was taking. DeeDee had schooled me to be aware of a thousand tiny details all at once, to know the path of every suspicious eye, but that day the rules of the game just seemed so stupid. So I wandered through the store, grabbing handfuls of designer lipstick, eyeshadow, and mysterious, ornate canisters of who-knows-what. Letting them all fly into my handbag with satisfying thuds, not looking over my shoulder or even down at the makeup. I wasn't looking at anything. And *thud, thud, thud.*

When DeeDee found me, I was alone in the Stila aisle with a fistful of lipliner. She grabbed my hips from behind and whispered in my ear urgently. "We're caught," she breathed. I couldn't see her, but a tendril of her yellow hair was curling around my shoulder. "Give me your purse," she said, "and get the hell out of here."

I didn't turn around, just shrugged my left shoulder, letting my bag slip into her open palm.

"I can't leave you," I said.

"Move," she said. "You know the drill. Twenty-five minutes." I was gone.

DeeDee and I had had an escape plan worked out since

we'd started at Montgomery Mall months earlier. Split up, run for our lives, and meet up at the bus stop by the Burger King, a quarter of a mile away. DeeDee, though, wasn't running. She was staying behind to take the rap, knowing that if she had my bag, with all the junk in it, they wouldn't be able to nail me.

So when the guard tried to stop me at the door, I just pushed past him. Everyone knows these mall security guards are just a step up from thieves themselves. Half a step. It's not like they're cops.

"Miss," the guard said, trying to block me with an arm. "You need to come with me."

"Sorry," I spat. And I ran. No one tried to follow. I powered down the phony mall boulevard, up the escalator, and through Hecht's, pushing through hordes of sluggish Christmas shoppers. The few times I looked over my shoulder, the place was deserted, a ghost town.

When I made it to the bus stop, I checked my watch every five minutes and watched the pavement horizon, shivering and waiting for the sight of DeeDee's blond, shattered halo flying down the sidewalk. It took twenty-five minutes, like she'd said. If she hadn't shown at that exact moment, I would have gone home by myself.

"Did I miss the bus?" she asked when she finally made it. She was hunching, out of breath, still unsteady on her heels.

"Two," I told her. "But you're still right on time. Twenty-five minutes."

"Well that's something, at least," she said, handing me

my purse. I glanced inside and was surprised to see that the makeup was still in it.

"How did you get out of there?" I wanted to know.

"I have my ways," she told me. "We just need to avoid that particular store for a little while."

"I shouldn't have left you," I said.

"I couldn't let you get in trouble, babe." She laughed, swinging her hair and hitting me on the butt with her purse. "You are too good for words." Then the bus showed up.

The smart thing would have been to stop stealing after that, or at least slow it down. But DeeDee believed that the smartest things to do were the ones that seemed at first to be the dumbest. So we kept on going and going.

In some ways I wish I could say that I was the one who started shoplifting for my brother. But it was Liz who first did it, one day in the beginning of November. The Gap was hopping with cheesy Christmas music, the Jackson Five chirping about Santa Claus, and Liz said to me: "God, the Jackson Five wig me out. To think that Michael was once thirteen himself." She shuddered theatrically.

I shrugged. DeeDee was busy in the dressing room, popping sensors off clothing while Liz and I stood in a corner in the back of the store behind a column of sweatpants. She was in a black tube top, her dark hair in a messy top-knot, and she stared at the ceiling while she talked, drumming her bright red fingernails absentmindedly against the wooden surface of a table stacked high with turtlenecks. When I didn't say anything about Michael Jackson, Liz just looked at me and grinned. She raised one eyebrow, and with a sly backhand, sent a pile of the shirts flying onto the floor. She left them lying there, then made a face and swiveled away from the mess, skintight jeans and black leather boots, beckoning for me to come with her. "What can I say?" she muttered. "At ten dollars an hour, they get what they pay for."

Liz led me to the cash register. "This one's for Jesse," she whispered as she dropped a royal blue lambswool v-neck into my dummy Bloomingdale's bag. He had a way of showing up in the conversation without any warning at all.

"He's not doing so good these days." I shrugged.

Liz looked both ways, then grabbed a pair of jeans off the rack. "Size one, right? All yours, Angel." She smiled sadly as she tossed them into my shopping bag. "If that brother of yours dies, I'm going to kill him. Return the pants if they don't fit."

DeeDee waltzed out of the dressing room, weighed down with booty. "Thanks, Liz." She grinned and took my hand in hers, sweeping me out of the store on a breeze. As we glided away, I could hear Liz saying to someone, "Oh, you must be mistaken. I know those girls."

Once Liz started taking shit for my brother, she didn't stop. The blue sweater, cheap Gap cologne, argyle socks, and the darkest, stiffest blue jeans. We visited her in the mall every day, and every day she'd drop the gifts in our bags or leave them hidden for us in the customer bathroom. The leather pants had been tricky, but she'd done it for Jesse, who was the first boy she'd ever kissed. Jesse, who was lying in a hospital bed where he had absolutely no use for leather pants, kept every item, always.

You might say that Liz was the one who really started me on stealing. Sure, DeeDee was my teacher. But without Liz I would never have had a purpose.

Leave it to DeeDee, though, to get it in an instant. When she found me for the first time, by the underpants in Abercrombie & Fitch and working charms on rows of tiny boxer-briefs, she knew immediately what I was doing. I had made half the underwear wall disappear. Disappearance, I had learned by then, was an easy art. It was more a way of thinking than anything else. All you had to do was swallow this pill of nothingness, and let the absence just course through your veins.

DeeDee was the only one who could always see me. That day she looked me up and down with a careful, appraising gaze. Her earrings were barely shuddering with the calm heaving of her cleavage. Breathe in, breathe out. As usual, I couldn't even meet her eyes. I wondered what I looked like to her.

"Underwear," she said. "Jesse will love it."

"It seems good for the hospital," I said. "So no one has to see your butt under that stupid gown they make you wear."

"Jesse has a great butt," DeeDee said.

"Ugh," I said. "Please, DeeDee. He's my brother."

I looked at the packages in front of me. The posters on the wall. These headless men with their smoothly etched muscles and tiny, flinty nipples. Hairless and big-chested enough to be women, except that they weren't. Maybe they were from a different universe, I thought. A more hearty universe where there was no such thing as a man or a woman, just these freaks in their underpants who were kind of both and kind of neither. And no need for the mess or the disease. They could just be in love with themselves. They could fuck themselves. Years later, I would wonder if DeeDee had come from that place too.

"Jesse's butt is not so great anymore, anyway," I told her. "What with him being a dead man and all. Not that I've thought about his butt ever."

"Well it's still a good present," DeeDee said breezily. "Make sure to tell him how much it all cost. A gift that is stolen means more because it really comes from the heart."

"So you've told me," I said.

"Stay here, babe. I'm going to go get him one of those puka-shell necklaces. He loves that surfer shit."

From then on, we stole only for Jesse, and did it with new precision. My boredom was gone. Instead, wherever I went, I hummed the tune of pumped-in mall Muzak. DeeDee and I stole with ponytails flying at our backs, with darting pupils and telltale rustling, hearts beating to the thump of high heels on fake marble tiles. We stole fishing lures and plastic charms and baseball caps and romance novels and crossword books like old ladies buy. All the time I was wondering, *"How do you rebuild a boy?"*

If anyone had the answer, I was sure, it was DeeDee. As long as I'd known her, there had never been a question that she could not answer.

It was her idea to get him the magazines, because that was the type of idea that she tended to have—a flawless combination of thoughtlessness and fucky insight. Staring at the forbidden top tier of the shelf in Crown books one day, she just smiled before twisting her mouth into a bratty pucker, and began tossing plastic-wrapped magazines into my bag, grabbing as many titles as she could without taking her sight off of the cold halogen track lighting on the ceiling. All blasé gum-pop and annoyed verve, eyes black and dull as asphalt. So of course it had been DeeDee's idea to take it, and of course she didn't panic when the bookstore clerks started giving us funny looks. Just raised her eyebrows and tilted her head to the side, jaw sharp and smooth as she blazed out of the store with me trailing behind.

DeeDee and I took the J12 to the hospital to give my brother his stuff.

"You don't have to come, you know," I told her.

"I'm not coming to be nice. I visit your brother cuz I'm in love with him."

It was true; she'd had a crush on him from the moment they met. And even though DeeDee was obsessed with beautiful things, she had somehow neglected to notice that Jesse was no longer handsome. Every time we saw him, it seemed like he had lost another part of his face, but DeeDee was just as smitten as ever. Was she just thoughtless, or was she seeing something else entirely?

"Hey, ya little thieves," Jesse said as we walked in.

"Hey, ya little faggot," said DeeDee. She knew he was just as in love with her as she was with him.

"Hi," I said. It all felt like small talk.

Jesse smiled at me. I smiled back, clenched-lipped, and shrugged, arching my eyebrows into a sheepish triangle.

"We brought you stuff." DeeDee pulled out one of the *Freshmen* and laughed. Jesse laughed. Then I laughed and we were all laughing. She tossed it onto his lap and he hid his face in his hands.

"My own little sister. What have I come to?"

"Check out page 12." DeeDee smirked. She smacked her fingers to her lips. "He's all mine."

"You guys are like too good to me. Too good and too young," Jesse said as he flipped through the magazine, eyes widening. Really, though, I could tell he was sad to see all those bodies, all young and sweaty and oozing—literally, you know—with life. DeeDee had made a miscalculation, but she didn't realize it. She never saw her own mistakes until they were penciled on notebook paper.

"You're welcome." DeeDee kissed Jesse on the forehead and left her glossy mark. He smiled—the old smile, almost. The careful upturn on one side of his lips. He was looking at me, not her. He looked like he was reading a book with a sad ending.

I examined my nail polish for chips, then looked up and narrowed my eyes at DeeDee, who was flipping through the magazines with Jesse and pointing out her favorites with her arm around his shoulders.

The next day in algebra I told DeeDee I couldn't go to the mall. "Too much shit to do," I wrote in the note I passed to her in the seat in front of me. We had gone to the mall after school every day since September except when she'd had the flu, so when she read that note she just turned around and raised one eyebrow at me. But she seemed cool with it.

I went to the hospital by myself, just because. When I got there I didn't even say hello, just climbed into Jesse's bed and curled up next to him.

"I don't think these beds are built for two," he said. "Believe me, I've tried."

"I'll fit," I said.

"Robin Hood," he murmured, "you are like so full of fearlessness that I can hardly stand it."

"And all this time I thought you knew what you were talking about," I said.

In the hospital bed I felt like a fetus, all pink translucence and no fingernails. If I was nine years older, I thought, Jesse and I could have been twins. But he was so much older than me. Old enough to be dying. My brother was nine when I was born and Jesse'd always been careless of that divide. He sent me to my room when he babysat so that he could screw sleazy ones on the floor of the family room. He left home for days at a time after fights with my stepfather. He always told me I was a stupid shit. But then at the beach he would carry me on his back, out beyond the waves where I'd float while he shaped my hair into salt-water sculptures, singing under his breath, "yellow is the color of my true love's hair."

This is nothing new, I know. This is an older brother.

I saw Liz one last time before Jesse died. Two days before, to be exact. I wasn't expecting her, because she was my brother's friend, not mine. And she was a grown-up, sort of. But she showed up on my doorstep on a chilly Sunday afternoon, asking for me. That day, Liz was dressed like an old-fashioned movie star, with a silk, polka-dotted scarf tied over her head and red cat's-eye sunglasses. But her lips were chapped and puffy bags peered out from the lower rims of her glasses. It looked retarded. Nice try, Liz, but sorry.

I tried to think of an excuse not to go with her, but I couldn't come up with one. So I got into her little blue Volkswagen, which had probably been paid for with hocked Gap merchandise, and we drove off.

She took me figure skating at the mall. Liz had been halfway decent at it once, when she was my age, but she'd given it up because her parents weren't about to pay for coaches and tutus and everything. It was just as well, Liz said. Who wants to be fat, insane, and broke, all for the sake of one triple axel at age sixteen?

"I'm moving to Australia soon," she said to me, when we were on the rink, just skating around and around, me grabbing her hip every now and then for balance. She had taken off the scarf and sunglasses as soon as we'd gotten out of the car.

"What are you going to do in Australia, of all places?" I asked her.

"I am going to break into the soaps. They're big there, you know. *Neighbours* and all. They call it *Naybas*. Maybe I'll meet a man with an Australian accent. It's all I ask."

"That's dumb," I told her.

"I know," she said. "Ridiculous, right? But something

ridiculous is the only thing left to do. And I love kanga-roos. So cute."

"When are you going?" I wanted to know.

"After—you know."

"After Jesse dies."

"Right." She did a little pivot on her skates, and sud-denly she was skating backward, facing me.

"Why are you telling me this?" I asked her.

"I wanted to say goodbye. Because when it happens, there's not going to be time. We're all going to be preoccu-pied over other stuff."

"I guess."

"It's going to be soon," Liz said. She took my hand and twirled me under the arch of her bicep. "I thought I could save him but I couldn't. It was so idiotic of us to suppose we could. There is no such thing as magic. Maybe we should have tried religion instead."

"Ha!" I said.

We'd done twenty or thirty laps of the rink at this point. We had passed this spot so many times that it seemed like we hadn't ever left it.

"You're not my sister, you know," I told the older girl.

"I sort of am," she said. "Jesse made me promise."

"Well he's not in charge," I said.

"I'd stay, but I can't," Liz said.

I hate it when people ignore me when I'm trying to be mean to them. But maybe she wasn't ignoring me.

"And what good am I anyway?" she went on. "I couldn't help Jesse. I spent years trying to help him, if you want the truth. Even before he got sick. Look where it got him. What makes him think I can look out for you?"

"The thing is that I don't know how to do anything except be a little sister," I told her.

"You know how to steal," she said.

"Like that counts." I snorted. But I realized that she was actually right.

"You won't be a little sister anymore," Liz told me. "You should get used to it because it's the truth. You'll see. You are as hard as diamond. You don't need us."

"Is that supposed to be a good thing?" I asked her.

"It's good," she said.

Then she left me, wobbling on the ice, to skate out to the eye of the rink, where there was a circle drawn for fanciness. There, Liz twirled and leapt while some old soft rock song played, narrowly dodging little kids and red-jacketed guards, while I retreated alone to the bleachers and smoked the first cigarette of my life. A Marlboro Light 100 bummed from an old lady.

I watched Liz skate. She had gone off like a bomb—detonated by a sequence of familiar twitches. She'd thought she wouldn't remember how to do it; she hadn't skated in years. But her body still knew, I guess, because she flew through the air with an instinct so killer that I was almost afraid to watch.

Liz stabbed the ice with the picks on her toes, threw her arms like helicopter blades before liftoff. Flakes of ice sparking from her feet. It reminded me, somehow, of DeeDee. I wondered if we'd always remember how to steal. I pictured myself, years in the future, reclaiming that sneaky art with a screaming baby in one hand and a bag of cat food in the other, in the crowded aisle of a supermarket. It would always be with me, I realized. For now, I could forget it if I wanted.

Jesse died two days later, around four in the afternoon. We'd basically known that he was going to croak that day, and we were all there. Me and Liz and Mom and Stepfather and Dad and even Max, who had been Jesse's boyfriend or whatever you want to call it. Everyone, even Stepfather who had hated Jesse, cried. Everyone except me. Liz seemed to understand. She held me tight, and I didn't even bother re-sisting, not at first at least. "I'll miss you," she said quietly. "Little sister."

"Don't call me that," I whispered. I pulled myself from her arms and headed to the elevator. I left the hospital and took the J12, not bothering to wait for anyone.

When I got home, I called DeeDee.

"I'm not going to school tomorrow," I told her when she picked up.

"Your brother died?" she asked.

"Yep."

"Does it suck?"

"I don't know," I said. "It's not like a surprise or any-thing."

"I have an English test tomorrow," she offered.

"That sucks," I said. I was feeling sickly flirtatious, lying on Jesse's bed and talking to DeeDee on the *Sports Illus-trated* football phone that someone had given to him as a joke. Jesse's room was an archaeological site, arranged in those layers: a record of him. I wondered if my mom was going to do that thing where she'd leave the room untouched, like a weird museum. That's what they always do on TV when a kid dies, but I didn't figure my mother for the type. She was too into decorating and home improvement. She'd probably spend a year stripping the paint on the windows, refinishing the floors and then turn the room into a study for Stepfather. We'd just see about that.

"We'll go to the mall," DeeDee's voice was echoing through the cheap plastic of the football phone. "You'll feel better."

"Now?" I asked, still disoriented by the room.

"No, tomorrow. I'll skip. That way you won't have to sit around the house all day."

"You sure?" I asked. "Didn't you skip your last English test too?"

"Yeah, but for you, baby. For you I'll skip another. I haven't read stupid *Midsummer Night's Whatever* anyway."

"You haven't missed much," I said. "In the end, nothing happened."

After I hung up, I rolled off of the bed and onto the floor where I lay for a minute eyeing the door. It was only then that I noticed a brown cardboard box sitting next to Jesse's desk. Crawling over, I opened it and found it all—the belongings of Jesse's that my mother had gathered up and brought back from the hospital. It wasn't all of his things. I don't know where the rest of it was; this box didn't have his real clothes or his cards or the paperbacks he had read when he couldn't do anything else. The box by his desk held only the things we had stolen for him. And they were all there, every one of those things—our tiny offerings. Here were the matching Minnie Mouse sweatbands from CVS. The underwear and Star Wars action figures. Here were the glittery jelly bracelets, the comic books, the aromatherapy candles, the porno, all of it. I couldn't believe that it all fit in just one box.

I called DeeDee back. "Will you sleep over?"

"I'll have to sneak out," she said. "Just cuz my mom's an alcoholic doesn't mean she'll let me sleep over on a Tuesday night."

"Obviously you say Jesse died," I told her.

"You got the hang of that pretty quickly," DeeDee said.

That night, my brother's room was still calling to us. All those mysterious drawers and crevices and old envelopes stuffed with gross letters—the dark places that had always been off-limits to a sister—were now mine by right. Jesse was gone and it felt like all the doors had been flung open.

"A dead man can't object to snooping," DeeDee said as she pulled a long forgotten bag of weed out from behind a book on the shelf. "It is, in fact, our solemn duty." We smoked the pot, not even worrying about someone smelling it, and went to sleep early in Jesse's bed.

"Why didn't you tell me you knew?" DeeDee asked. "I should have been there too. At the hospital."

"You're not his sister," I said.

"Well neither is Liz," DeeDee said.

When I woke up, the girl and I were wrapped in each other, gripping tight.

And please imagine the following in pink ballpoint pen. With bubbles to dot the *i*'s except that there are no *i*'s. Please imagine the following in tight, bouncy script, with letters crammed tight and edge to edge like there is a shortage of paper. This is DeeDee's handwriting. The last item in that tiny red notebook. The End. *We went to the mall.*

Bloomingdale's was the northern fortress, protected by guards and watchful clerks and cameras and store detectives. DeeDee and I had never hit it before; we'd been saving it for a special occasion. The day after Jesse died we descended on it like secret agents—with rubber bands in our pockets and old Saks bags in place of our little black purses. As a joke we wore our most mysterious sunglasses and the darkest lipstick. We dressed all in black, including huge wide-brimmed hats, as was appropriate for women in mourning. DeeDee forged the way like she always had, dropping everything into her Saks bag without a thought.

DeeDee and I went to the mall and you knew from looking at us that we were something else. Cool and tall, invincible, beautiful. Valkyries—opposites, but clearly sisters. In Bloomingdale's the tables were overflowing with things that I took: comfortable wool sweaters, long, scented candles and bottles of translucent blue bubble bath, a set of good cutlery and a Belgian waffle iron with six settings. Jesse was dead and didn't need anything more. With Jesse gone I only took things for myself. And what was the point? I was just going to throw it away. What was the point, because it wasn't going to help me anyway. But there must have been a point, because I went a little overboard.

"I think Julia Child is my shopping partner," DeeDee said as we went down the escalator to Intimates. "What do you want with fancy cooking knives?"

"I just like them. They're sharp, okay?"

"Maybe you shouldn't take anything else. You've got a good haul," DeeDee said.

"Maybe you should leave me alone," I told her. "Maybe you got me into this in the first place."

We didn't say anything after that, but we both knew how it was. Walking through the racks of bras, we were so quiet. Then we were caught.

For once, she was the one who was blindsided; for once I was the one who saw the security guards, out of uniform and aiming for us in sharky strides. I caught my breath and looked over at DeeDee, who seemed, in that glance, suddenly so unimpressive. Even in her enormous hat. She couldn't protect me, and there was really no use in trying to protect her. And there it was.

It was DeeDee's idea to start stealing.

DeeDee taught me how to steal. But what did she know? I would never be like her. There was no way anyone could match her absurd gift: that white-hot dazzle that obscured the fact that she was no different from any ordinary girl.

DeeDee, I thought, *go ahead, be the sun. Everyone knows there is only room for one in any solar system anyway.*

And it didn't matter. Because I was something more mysterious. I was a shadow; a shadow; a shadow.

"Hold my bag for a sec, Dee," I said as the guards got closer. "I have to go to the bathroom."

"Sure, babe," she said, absentmindedly, sticking out her arm without even looking up from a rack of lacy thongs. The next time we would speak, I mean really speak, was three and a half years later.

But I dropped my bag into her hand and turned quick, bolting for the door, which was only a few feet away. As I passed under the glowing red EXIT sign I looked back for a second and saw my best friend staring back at me, panicking as the guards rifled through the loot she held: four bags filled to the top. Through racks of frilly underwear, DeeDee's mascara'd lashes were stunned and spidery; her lips were petrified in a half-kiss. I was not scared. I just looked away and ran. But for the tiniest moment before I swiveled, I saw Jesse again, standing next to DeeDee with his hand on her shoulder. "Fearless," he had said to me once. "You are like so fearless."

In Jesse's bed, the night before, DeeDee gripped me tight as we fell asleep. Skinny arms around my waist, perfect chest against mine, and her knees tucked tight against her belly. Without the high heels and towering ponytail, she was actually very small. That night, I had been drifting off when she'd grabbed my wrists and started shaking. Like a blade of grass or a tiny bug. I can't promise you that I wasn't dreaming when it happened, but either way I'd felt the girl crying into the bare curve of my neck. My brother was dead and DeeDee was just the softest buzz. That night her warm breath was steady in my ear; that night she'd whispered to me in our sleep. What she said changes every time I try to remember. I guess you could say that I wasn't listening. Honestly, I didn't care enough to hear. What could she have told me that I didn't already know?

The Last Second

A. M. Jenkins

The air in the living room was warm and sleepy. Blaine was warm and sleepy, too. The sun came through the window behind him, making a square patch of light on the floor, so bright that it threw everything around it into a dim haze.

He couldn't have said how long he'd been there, sitting on the faded couch with its back against the window. He had a feeling that there was something he was supposed to be doing, but his mind was fuzzy and not awake.

He sat drowsing, watching the dust motes rise, drift, and fall. For a while he looked at the familiar room around him, the scratched surface of the coffee table, the sketches and prints scattered on the walls, the wide doorway that led into the kitchen. When his mother appeared on the other side of it, he watched her as she absentmindedly dabbed a damp sponge at spots on the counter.

When he turned his attention back to the rich tones of the wooden floorboards in the golden square of sun, he saw that the square had changed a little, grown longer and thinner.

The feeling rose in him, a little stronger: There was something he needed to do.

In the kitchen, his mother's face wore a strange, pinched look, her eyes red and the tip of her nose raw. She did not look at him, but fished a wad of Kleenex from her pocket and scrubbed at her nose. She didn't speak.

Blaine did not speak, either. Now he noticed that the square of sunlight had not only turned into a rectangle, it had also moved. It was sliding across the floor at a slow pace that marked the passage of daylight.

He felt the barest press of panic. Night was coming again.

It was a familiar feeling. *That* was sharp and clear— how, when he was a kid running outside for one more chance to play after supper, his mom would tell him to "be in before dark." How, when he felt the hot summer asphalt growing cooler under his bare feet, he would interrupt his play to check the sky with dread, watching the stark bright light paling to steal the day away. Even though he was little, he knew what was coming: shadows and silence and aloneness.

Now he looked at the thinning line of sun, and told himself: *It's only night. Just another night—it's nothing. You're too old to be afraid.*

He remembered it had started long ago, after they'd moved, because the new house was so big, and his bedroom was at one end of the house, while his parents' was at the other. It was a long silent way to another human being after bedtime. He'd clutch his beloved stuffed cat to him, but the small comforting body somehow in the dark became lifeless and limp—no help at all. Alone at night, the stillness pressed on him till he felt as if he was in a box with the lid unmoving against his face and chest. He could not get enough breath into his lungs, and somehow he would be out of bed before he knew it, and stumbling down the stairs, shaking and crying.

Now, as he waded into alertness, darkness loomed at the edge of the weakening sunlight, worked its way across the floor toward him. It would not yield, would not pause, would not be ignored or shoved aside.

Not until he figured out what it was he had to do.

His mother had given up wiping the counter. The sponge lay there, forgotten, while she absently straightened some cards and letters that were stacked next to the phone. The paper rustled, moving through her fingers. She did not seem to know that he was there.

It struck him suddenly that this all was very familiar. It was as if he'd done it before, as if he had already woken from the same sleepy daze, to this same realization that night was coming, the same inescapable dread. As if he'd sat in this exact spot more than once, having these exact thoughts.

Now he felt the facts growing around him, a shadow hardening into shape: His mother? This was what she did every day. Mindless chores, then she would forget what she was doing, or lose heart, and wander off, leaving the chore unfinished.

This was what she had been doing, every day for days.

How many days? He did not know. All he knew—and he didn't know how he knew it—was that his mother would not look at him. She would not speak to him. And when the sun left, he would be alone.

Right now, on the couch, he could see by the shrinking bit of sun that he had already wasted a lot of time. The remaining light had become blunted and deadened. The day had almost completely flowed past him—and he had to figure out what was required of him, before the sunlight went completely away.

All the nights knit themselves together like a badly sewn patchwork that pressed unseen from all sides, squeezing him. In the kitchen, his mother had opened one of the cards and was reading it. He could not make out the design on the front, but he could feel the idea of it; a lone, somber something, and the spidery trailing letters above it had a sense of sorrow about them.

A sympathy card, Blaine thought. And he knew that he was right, as surely as he felt the sunlight rolling inexorably along.

Sympathy for what?

He looked down at the bronze-colored velvet of his parents' old couch, the same one they'd had ever since he was a kid. These were the same cushions he'd stacked on the floor, flinging himself, face-first, onto the pancaked pile. He recalled that weightless, joyful moment of flight before gravity bore him down.

But now as he looked, he realized that the cushions he'd thought he was sitting on were empty, and smooth—not even an indentation. The couch was a wide expanse unbroken by his body.

He was not there. He could see, but he was not there. His mother would not speak to him because she could not perceive him, and that was because he no longer was physically present.

I'm dead. The thought didn't surprise him. As soon as it presented itself, he knew that he realized this same truth every night. It was an unrelenting truth, solid and unmoving as granite; he could feel how true it was.

He watched his mother read through the cards and letters. Panic and grief rose in a rush—but he had to push them down. They were too strong, they might carry him off, and there was no time. He was alone, no one could see or hear or help, and night was coming on.

The answers were inside himself somewhere, he could feel it. He had to remember. He had to figure this out.

He cast about for some memory of dying. All he could pull out were bits and snatches. Like the oddly muffled sound of the siren, from inside the ambulance. The plastic mask clamped over his nose and mouth, which seemed to make it harder, not easier, to breathe. In the emergency room, curt voices calling orders, lights so bright they felt like they were stabbing into his eyes.

The phone rang. His mother did not move. She remained leaning over the counter, staring at the letters and cards now spread before her as the phone rang and rang, almost under her hand, harsh in the quiet.

Finally, the answering machine kicked on.

"Hey."

It was his father.

"Looks like I'm going to be working a little late tonight."

That was Dad, all right. Reliable as Old Faithful, with a work ethic that didn't bend, not even for the death of his son.

"Don't hold dinner for me. I'll probably be up here till at least ten."

Ten was late, even for Dad. This was familiar, too; his father putting in as many hours as possible, trying to avoid the grief that had worn grooves into the air of the house.

All of it was familiar to Blaine. He realized now that he too, was wearing grooves into the air; the same thing, every day. Every day he woke to slow awareness in the sun that crept like unrelenting clockwork across the floor; every day he watched the house, saw his mother; every day he remembered that he was dead.

Over and over and over.

The reason?

He had to. He had to keep repeating it until he figured out what he was supposed to do. Was it his punishment? Had he done something wrong?

Remember, remember. Before the ambulance ride. What happened then?

It had been raining. He remembered the drops splattering the windshield—yes, he had been driving. He was angry, he remembered that—angry about a trivial something that he couldn't recall. Grades, maybe? Mom had lectured him, and he had stomped out of the house.

Rain pattering on the roof of the car. Drops on the

windows. The *thuh-thunk* of the wipers. The gush of water under the wheels.

There had been a stop sign. He remembered that, seeing the sign too late, the slow-motion realization that the brakes were not responding to his commands. Because of the rain? Or had he been drinking?

No, he hadn't been drinking. He was just angry, that was all; angry about nothing, and driving too fast in the rain.

He did not remember the driver of the other car at all, but the backseat—in the backseat he could still see it, a small head visible just above the car door; a child's face turned toward him, growing closer and closer, eyes widening with terror, mouth opening in an inaudible cry.

Then everything had been swept away by the sound of twisting metal and breaking glass. But that little boy was dead, too. He had to be. It had been like a bad dream. Unreal. Like a movie.

Maybe that was it; he had to feel the realness of it. Or maybe he had to feel whatever it was that little boy felt before *he* died.

Yes. This wasn't about *doing*. It was about *understanding*. There was something he was supposed to *understand*. All he had to do was figure it out, and he'd be free.

But what? That he'd caused someone else to die? Was he supposed to say that he was sorry? That he was responsible? But *he'd* suffered every bit as much as that kid! *He* was dead, too!

The sunlight was a mere slit now. He felt the anger rising again. How much time was left? Minutes? Seconds?

This whole thing was unfair. It wasn't his fault, it was the rain, the slick road. And his mom, she'd lectured him, she was the one who'd made him mad, made him careless. And the other car shouldn't have pulled out in front of him like that, it should have seen that he wasn't going to be able to stop.

He hadn't really done anything wrong. He'd just been careless for the briefest of moments—just a tiny bit reckless, that's all.

With that thought, the slit of sunlight disappeared from the floor. His anger turned into anguish. The fading had begun, like it always did.

He would spend another night alone in silence, and in the dark.

The gloom ate the last dusky bit of sunlight. The familiar living room faded till there was no clock, no sound, not even a ragged breath or heartbeat. The air around him grew heavy and the thick darkness swallowed everything till it was solid like earth.

Alone for the Weekend

Martin Wilson

On a Saturday morning in November, Alex finds himself alone for the weekend, so he decides to break a few rules. First, he wears his father's silk navy-blue robe around the house and turns the thermostat up. He doesn't flush the toilet right away or put the seat down, nor does he take the trash out, just lets all the debris—balled-up napkins, fast-food bags and paper cups, a clunky box of stale cereal—pile and cling close to the edges. Last night he ate a cheeseburger and an order of fries with ketchup mixed with mayonnaise on his parents' wedding china, and he didn't even wash the plate afterward, just let it sit on the counter, the crumbs and salt caking on the grease. He also drank five Heinekens from the basement refrigerator, and some of his older brother's stash of cheap vodka from a large, green-tinted plastic bottle, which his brother hides in his old toy chest under his soccer gear.

The weekend wasn't supposed to be a solitary one, but his older brother, James, has also broken rules: After their mother and father left for their weekend getaway to the beach house on the Gulf—leaving numbers for them to call in case of an emergency, money for meals—James went to stay with his girlfriend at the La Quinta Inn by the interstate. He told Alex that he had planned this La Quinta weekend for a while. *Don't fuck it up for me,* he said. James's girlfriend is named Alice, but the name doesn't suit her, Alex thinks, because Alices are usually maids or Sunday school teachers or sweet-faced TV weather girls. He has seen this Alice at school—she's a senior, like James—and Alex knows that she doesn't wear a bra, she says "Jesus Fucking Christ," and she smokes Marlboro cigarettes. Alex is certain that she has had other boys to the La Quinta before, James isn't so special.

So, a whole day alone, and Alex doesn't feel like doing much of anything. No homework, no letter writing, no pleasure reading, nothing. Mostly he sits around. Sometimes it gets too quiet and he hears the house settling in pops and cracks, so he turns on the TV or the radio for company.

Outside, the grass of the front lawn is beige and brittle, the pine trees thin and naked, the limbs of the oaks an exposed pale gray, and Alex can see houses and windows that are normally hidden by foliage in the spring or summer or fall. In the house across the street, a light burned all night long in an upstairs window. Alex knows this because he stayed up almost all night, peering out his own window, scrutinizing the cars that drove by at three in the morning, watching house lights flicker on and mostly off in the neighboring homes, listening to an occasional dog bark and the random sounds of night. Now Alex stands in the kitchen, picks at a powdered doughnut he has plucked from a plastic package, and looks out the window at the same house and sees the small boy who lives there with his mother. The renters, Alex's mother calls them. The little boy has red hair, extremely red, the unnatural color of a Coke can. He lies in his driveway without a coat on and reads a heavy book. Alex often sees this little boy outside, lurking, talking to himself, moving his hands about like a conductor, always alone, like he is today.

The phone rings—an angry, intrusive noise—and Alex stands there and thinks about not answering it. The little boy, as if he can hear it ringing, picks up his head and stares at Alex's yard. Alex answers it quietly. Before his parents left, they told him that if anyone called for them to tell whoever it was that they were busy or out running errands, not out of town. In case a potential robber or kidnapper or killer called and got some ideas.

"May I speak to the man of the house, please." A female voice, overly formal, practiced.

"He's out of town." Another broken rule, but it doesn't matter—it's just a woman from the phone company and she says she'll call back at a more convenient time.

He hadn't thought the phone would be for him anyway, because no one has called Alex for months, ever since he swallowed Pine-Sol at Marty Miller's lake house party and had to be rushed to the hospital. The party—the annual welcome-back-to-school drunk fest—had been ruined, and after it happened everyone thought Alex was mentally disturbed. Fucked in the head. In the weeks after the party, Alex—out of school for two weeks—sat at home waiting for the phone to ring, waited for his friends Kirk and Tyler—his musketeers, his mother always called them—and the others to call him. For some gesture of concern, at least from the girls like Beth or Lang or Susan. Girls are supposed to be sweet and caring like that. But they never called, and that's not all—they avoid him at school. They nod at him without meeting his eyes, and he can almost hear their thoughts about him as he continues down the halls: freak, loser, stay away from us, thank you very much.

James thinks Alex is crazy and has said as much. At the hospital, while their parents talked to the hospital psychiatrist in the hall, James said, "Why would anyone do that? Why? There was beer at that party, why didn't you just drink the beer for Christ's sake?"

And Alex wanted to answer him, but he just fingered his identification bracelet and watched the empty gray-green screen of the TV that was perched on a ledge in the corner of the room. If only he could have transported himself into the TV, into some after-school special, where a boy like him, after an event like this, could return home, return to school, triumphantly in the fiftieth minute of the show, all forgiven, all misunderstandings cleared, credits rolling.

After the party, Alex's mother locked all of the cleaning supplies in her bathroom cabinet, using an actual padlock, even though Alex swore that they didn't need to worry about him doing something like that anymore. So after a few weeks they got rid of the padlock. After all, couldn't Alex just buy more on his own if he really wanted to do it again? It was ridiculous, locking it all away. But still, though unlocked, his mother hides all toxic supplies behind boxes of Kleenex, rolls of Charmin. His mother didn't even want to go to the beach this weekend. But James assured her that he would see that nothing happened. He had promised. Besides, as Alex's father said, after all they had been through they both deserved a vacation. And so they had left with their weekend bags after giving rigid goodbye hugs.

On this Saturday, Alex has taken the Mr. Clean (as if, somehow, a different brand would be enough of a deterrent) out from under the dusty cabinet and placed it on the kitchen counter next to the blender.

Outside, the little redheaded boy is throwing pebbles at a neighbor's iron mailbox, which is painted to look like a cozy, two-story lime-green house, complete with a shingled roof and a flagstone walkway. Alex's own house is redbrick, two-story, rectangular, pretty but not an architectural wonder, though the bricks were brought in special from a torn-down eighteenth-century hospital all the way up in Virginia—his father is so proud of this, but Alex thinks all bricks look the same. The backyard backs up to a small thatch of forest, and in the front yard there is a low, pocked oak tree that he used to climb but doesn't anymore. The backyard has a swing set that hasn't been used for some time now, but which is still rooted in the ground with concrete. Alex's mother wants to build a gazebo where the swing set is, but his father is dragging his feet about it. He thinks about all this now, the particulars of his home, and he realizes he has lived in this house his whole life. He thinks, maybe for the first time, how odd this is, that these walls and this carpet, these bug-littered windowsills, these trees and these doors—they are the only ones he has ever known. And yet it doesn't feel like it used to, it doesn't feel familiar—something is different, and the silence only reminds him of this. He even smells his house—the way only strangers can smell other peoples' houses. It is a sour smell, like a lemony sweat, fruity scented from the dried fruit bits his mother places out in dishes all over the place.

The phone rings again and he grabs it immediately. He doesn't say hello, but holds his mouth there, as if waiting to kiss it.

"Hello?" a voice says. The same woman.

"No one's home," he says and hangs up.

Alex showers and changes clothes but continues to wear the robe over a pair of jeans and a purple T-shirt that advertises the bank his father works for: FIRST ALABAMA BANK—YOU CAN COUNT ON US! While outside the noon sun tries to slip through the stubborn clouds, he sits on his bed like he is waiting for something to happen. He eyes a stack of books on the floor next to his desk, school textbooks covered with brown grocery-bag paper that he has doodled on. His wire-bound notebooks are also filled with doodles, and a few scribbled sentences inside, often incomplete. Alex opens the yellow history notebook, and sees a page that is dated two months ago to the day. On the page, in his neat print, he reads "WEEKEND PLANS" in thick inky strokes. But no plans are listed. He used to make lists all the time, lists that outlined what he needed to do, what he wanted to do, what his parents wanted him to do, what he would like to buy, what books he should read to better himself. So many lists, so much plotting out. When he accomplished a goal that he had written down, he would take a red felt-tip pen and draw a line through the words. Then he felt like he had accomplished something. But he has stopped making the lists because he feels that there's nothing that he needs to do, nothing important in life anymore except making it to the next day. At night in bed he's relieved the day's over, and right when he wakes up in the morning, still groggy, he experiences quick spurts of excited happiness, but that's before he's fully awake, before he realizes a whole day like all the others before it stretches in front of him.

In the living room, he looks outside once again and sees that the small child is still out there, walking on the curb as if negotiating a balance beam. Alex wants to go outside to check the mail, even though he knows none of it will be for him. But he doesn't want to have to look at the child, doesn't want to nod his head or say hello as neighbors should. That requires too much. He wishes the boy would go inside to eat lunch or something. He suddenly remembers that the child's name is Henry, which he knows because a few weeks ago the child's mother—a woman with curly sandy hair who likes to wear suede jackets with matching frilly boots— hung a large neon orange banner across the garage that read HAPPY 10TH B-DAY HENRY! The day after, Alex saw the child on a ladder taking it down, while the mother, wine-glass in hand, watched from the kitchen door.

Alex decides to check the mail anyway—he will just have to keep his eyes glued to the walkway until he is safely back through the front door. He walks downstairs and pulls open the door and it sticks a moment, then squeaks open. The air is cold and smells of wood burning from fire-places. The sun is trapped behind the clouds—it might as well give up. He walks to the mailbox self-consciously be-cause he knows he's being watched. And just as he feared, Henry talks to him.

"Hey there."

Alex nods without looking at him.

"Why are you wearing a robe?" the boy asks.

Alex looks at the child, who stands on the opposite curb. He is wearing black church pants and a yellow sweat-shirt with no logo and is holding the large book against his chest. The book wears no jacket, is clothbound red, and even from a few feet away Alex can see that it is heavily dog-eared. The child's mouth is open like he is preparing to swallow something and he is scratching the inside of one of his ears.

"Because I feel like it," Alex says, reaching and opening the mailbox, which is empty.

"I could've told you that the mailman hasn't come yet," the child says.

"Well, now I know," he says, and in a sudden fit of irri-tation that surprises him, Alex asks, "Why have you been outside all day long?" He turns to face the kid only briefly, then looks back to the mailbox, into which he peers deeper, as if hoping that a letter will appear out of thin air to prove the kid wrong.

"I just want to," Henry answers.

"It's not even a nice day. And what's with the book?"

"Oh. Well, I'm reading the dictionary because my mother says that it's never too early for a kid my age to sharpen his vocabulary."

"That's nice," Alex says, but what it really is, he thinks, is weird. He turns to walk inside.

"You're going in?" Henry says.

"What?" Alex says, tightening his eyes.

"Do you know what *smalto* is?"

"What? No, of course not," Alex says.

"It's colored glass. Like they have in churches. I just learned that."

"You're just ten; you shouldn't be reading the dictionary. You should be playing or something. Whatever you kids do nowadays." Like he is so old himself, a hardened adult or something, though he is only sixteen.

"Play with who?" Henry asks. "I don't know any kids in this neighborhood."

It's true—the neighborhood is old, full of doctors with children away at college, or professors from the university with teenagers, retired lawyers with grandchildren who never visit, no new, young families. There used to be kids, of course, but everyone has aged and remained in the same houses. He stares at the child, shakes his head. "We have a swing in our backyard," he says, almost not believing his own words. "You can come use it if you want." The child nods at him as if mulling it over, then steps across the street, already accepting the offer. For a moment Alex is uncertain what to do, but then he shuts the mailbox with a clank and walks up to the front door, and out of the corner of his eye he sees the flash of red hair galloping beside him.

Alex must lift up his legs because he's too tall and gangly for the swing. The blue plastic seat strains underneath him, pulls into a tight U, pinches his hips. Henry sits in the swing next to his, a perfect fit. They both cut through the air, and because of the combined weight, the back end of the swing set sometimes lurches out of the ground. Alex imagines swinging high enough so that the swing set gets completely yanked out of the ground, sending him and the child sprawling and laughing onto the grass.

"You have very red hair. It's not natural," Alex says, in flight.

"I like it. My mother did it. I told her I wanted red hair, not orange hair. Everyone said I had red hair, but that wasn't really true. Mom said she could make my hair really red if I wanted."

"Well, it looks funny," Alex says.

"I like it," Henry says again, tossing his head back as he rises into the air.

"I do too, in a weird way," Alex says. His own hair is light brown and short, shaved close to his scalp so that he hardly ever needs to brush it. James told him he looked like a dying sick person with such a haircut. It hasn't grown out yet. James's hair is thick and he is growing it long because that's the way Alice likes it, but Alex thinks James looks ridiculous with it, like a shaggy terrier.

"Where are your parents?" Henry asks.

"On a trip."

Alex slows down and hops out of the swing and Henry follows him onto the back deck. Alex almost wants to tell him to go away, that their time together—twenty minutes of swinging—is over, but then he remembers the smell of the house, the electric silences of it, and decides that company would be okay for a while, but just for a while.

Alex is hungry, but because there is not much food in the house, and because he hasn't felt like going to the grocery, he settles for whatever he can find, which happens to be crackers and butter, and which he shares on a plate with Henry. They sit on the blue couch in the living room—where food of any kind is usually forbidden—and from their adjacent seats they can see Henry's house across the street. It's an ugly and unkempt, two-story (all the houses on his street are) house of painted-gray brick, with a gray-tiled roof, with overgrown and dying boysenberry bushes covering many of the front windows. It used to be a nice place, when the pediatrician lived there with his wife, but Henry's mother, a renter, doesn't bother to cut the lawn, doesn't bother to repaint the cracking paint of the trim, leaves the garbage can on the curbside even after it has been picked up. But the house is large, and Alex wonders what Henry and his mother do with so much unneeded space. Why would they rent such a house?

Henry presses his knife that holds one square of butter down too hard on the cracker, causing it to fracture like a sheet of ice.

"What happened to your father?" Alex asks.

Henry places the cracker into his mouth and doesn't speak again until he has chewed and swallowed. "Mom says that I don't have one," he says.

"You have to have one. Someone, somewhere."

Henry shrugs. "I don't know. She never talks about him. She doesn't like it when I ask her. So I don't."

Alex stares out at the house, tries to remember if he has even seen any other cars parked there, early in the morning, or late at night, and he is sure he has. Boyfriends maybe.

"You must be happy to have a brother," Henry says.

"I guess," Alex says. But the truth is, Alex hasn't felt comfortable around James for some time now. He remembers when they used to walk in the woods together, constructing forts in ditches, forts out of downed tree limbs and pine needles that they could escape to and hide in if the Russians ever attacked, if their parents ever died and the orphanages came after them. But that was when they were kids. When he was Henry's age and younger. He could laugh with James then, back when James looked him in the eyes and back when Alex could return such a look without feeling he was being intrusive. Without feeling the need to apologize for something. That was so long ago, before James liked girls and became concerned about his muscles.

"Does he tell you dirty jokes?"

"Sometimes. He has a girlfriend named Alice. He's with her right now."

"I read this book about two brothers and one was always telling the other one dirty jokes. I thought if I had a brother we could do that."

Alex closes his eyes and leans back in his seat, resting his head. He doesn't know why, but what Henry has just said has made him feel overwhelmingly sad. The same feeling of sadness he got the time he saw one of the janitors outside in the parking lot after school. It had been a windy day, and the janitor, overweight in a huff-and-puff-breathing and doughy way, had his hat blown off by the wind and he chased it across the lot, bending just in time for the wind to carry it away again, and how Alex's friends, observing just as he was, sitting on their car trunks, had laughed at the man and said, "Fat fucker." Then they had yelled it so the janitor could hear, though he pretended he hadn't. That was before the Pine-Sol, of course. He hadn't thought of the janitor when he swallowed, but it seems to him now that he should have been thinking about such things. Actually, he can't remember what he was thinking about then. James had even asked him, "What were you thinking?" No, he had said, "Man, what the hell were you thinking?"

Henry drops the knife on the carpet with a light thud. "Oops."

Alex picks it up and asks Henry, "Have you ever had vodka?"

Henry laughs and says, "No, I'm a kid."

Eyes still closed, he says, "Sorry. I forgot." But he hadn't—he is quite aware that Henry is a child.

On the back deck, Alex sits on a lawn chair, holding James's bottle of vodka. James was always good about sharing his booze, at least. "I'd rather you drink that than floor wax," James said when Alex had asked him for a drink a few weeks after he came home from the hospital. In the days before Alex swallowed Pine-Sol, James had shown him how to mix drinks that tasted good—sour, fruity drinks of bright color, or milky, sugary ones. When he had first thrown up from drinking, James was there to give him a hot towel to wipe his face with. He had thrown up after the Pine-Sol too, burning his throat so bad he couldn't open his eyes. And then they had pumped his stomach, shoved a tube down his nose and throat, and he kept his eyes closed then too.

Henry sits down on a wrought iron chair and drinks from a small glass of Coke with a half a lime in it. "That stuff smells," Henry says, pointing with his glass to the vodka bottle. "My mother doesn't touch it anymore. She used to though."

"Vodka doesn't smell," Alex says, remembering that he had heard that somewhere. But Henry is right, it does stink. "Anyway, one day you'll learn that it makes you feel good."

"My mother only drinks wine."

Alex thinks of his own mother, and also of his father. He can see them on the beach: She is reading a cheap, worn-edged paperback novel, he is lying on his stomach, snoring, with a lightly sunburned back. Or perhaps they are sitting on the deck of the beach house, sipping drinks, facing the Gulf, talking and lounging, just as he and Henry sit on this back porch. Two months ago, after the incident, Alex

spent a week at that beach house with his parents. His father wanted him to get some rest. Alex had his nearly
shoulder-length hair then. Lang, a girl friend from school,
had told him that he had beautiful hair and that it would
be a shame if he never let it grow out. For eight months he
had let it grow. His bangs covered his eyes and the sides
hung over his ears like tassels. But that night on the deck of
the beach house, Alex cut his hair with some scissors he had
found in the kitchen drawer. "I just don't know what's
wrong with him," he heard his mother tell his father the
next morning, after she had seen his shorn head. "I just
don't." And Alex had walked along the beach that day, the
still-strong September sun burning his once-hidden forehead.

"Alex, are you drunk?" Henry asks.

"No," Alex replies. But he is.

"My mother didn't come home last night," Henry says.

Alex drinks some more from the bottle, closing his eyes
as he swallows.

"I stayed up for her, but she didn't come home. She
stays out on Friday night a lot. At her boyfriend's place. But
she usually comes home by now. Or calls me."

Alex looks at Henry, this ten-year-old boy with red hair
who wears a yellow sweatshirt and black pants. "You look
like the German flag," he says. It's something he would say
only while drinking.

Henry looks at him quizzically. "I hate my house when
it gets dark outside," he says.

"I'm still hungry," Alex says. "Want to go somewhere?
Go for a ride?"

Henry nods yes, looking up into the darkening sky, like something awful is floating his way.

Alex drives his mother's Volvo, not his own Honda Civic. It's a bigger car, but smooth and fast. He drives to the mall but decides not to stop because it's crowded.

"I hate the mall," Henry says.

"Me too," Alex says, but he doesn't hate it as much as he hates all the people there and the easy chance of running into someone he knows. The town's like that—you'll run into people everywhere. When he eats out with his parents, they can't make it through the restaurant without having to stop to talk with some acquaintances. His mother always introduces him to people he's met ten times already, people he's seen at church every Sunday or at James's soccer games.

Alex drives past other strips of shops, past a string of chain restaurants whose lots are depressingly full, past the hospital where he was born, which is modernized now with a new whitewashed wing. A big Christmas tree is perched and lit in front of the new wing, in the patch of grass before the circular drive to the main doors. It's only November, not even Thanksgiving, but already this early celebration. Alex can't even remember what he got for Christmas last year, and he hasn't asked for anything this year. His mother has talked about spending the holiday at the beach house, for a change, but no one else seems enthused about it.

He drives into neighborhoods off the main streets, narrow lanes of dull-painted ranch tract houses with yellowed crabgrass, tucked cozily away from the busier roads. How odd that he's never been down these streets before.

"Are you ever going to stop?" Henry asks. Alex sees the clock and realizes he has been driving now for thirty minutes.

He turns around and goes back the way they came, past the bridge over the small, muddy Black Warrior River, and soon he sees Burger King up ahead. It's the same Burger King where, months ago, he hung out with his friends. It was such a small-town thing to do, but it was a good place to collect before going to the parties. They'd park their cars, turn up their stereos, buy big paper cups of Coke or Sprite and then mix alcohol into them.

He was there the night he swallowed Pine-Sol. That night. He remembers that everyone seemed to be ignoring whatever he said, how Kirk had told him his taste in music sucked. The way Susan couldn't stop saying "Like I give a shit, sweetie." There was the smell of unsmoked Camel cigarettes, the drops of whiskey and Coke that he had spilled on his leather shoes. From Burger King they went to the party, out on the winding roads to the lake, down a curvy hill where they had to park on a muddy shoulder. Walking down the hill, he could hear the lake waters slap against the wood of the docks. The house was big and made of dark wood, and inside it was decorated with mix-and-match furniture that Marty Miller's mother had rejected from her "real" house—pea-green couches, wicker side tables, lamps made from logs. Alex remembers a musty smell inside, the crowd, the blaring stereo that kept being turned on and off while people fought over which music to play. He drank cups of beer from the keg, walked around the house, felt invisible, never could seem to find his friends and when he did they never really paid him much attention. What had brought about this change? One minute he had felt a part of something, and the next he felt like he had been let go without having been told why. A fired employee, a bride left at the altar, all without explanation.

He continued to drink. Then things get foggy in his mind. He was in one of the back bathrooms, he had just peed, and in the medicine cabinet, instead of finding pills or Band-Aids, he found the Pine-Sol. He remembers the burning throat after he took the swig. He took more than one swig, though each swallow was hard, much harder than taking a shot of cheap tequila, as he had done earlier. The burn. Like little needle pricks down his throat. Then vomiting, and more burning. Someone opening the door to the bathroom—he hadn't locked it. He remembers a lot of cussing from his classmates and a blond girl he didn't know who kept calling him Alan and asking what his last name was, last name, I need your last name! Commotion, the awed faces jolted out of flirting and boozing into something surreal. The paramedics, and then the bizarre stares of anguish he got from his parents. The hospital psychiatrist, a pinched-looking man trying so hard to be kind. His throat took weeks to heal, and he always associates the weeks after the party with Jell-O and canned soup and salt-water gargles.

Coming up on Burger King, he almost passes it by, but at the last second he turns into the parking lot. "Is this okay?" he asks Henry.

"I don't have any money."

"I'll spot you."

Henry nods his head.

Alex sits in the car a moment before shutting it off. He scans the lot for familiar cars—Lang's bumper-stickered (MEAN PEOPLE SUCK) Jeep, Tyler's inherited blue Volkswagen station wagon, nicknamed the Blue Goose because of its funny honk. But none of their cars are here—the coast is clear.

They get out and enter the heat and fried smell of the place. Mostly solitary diners on this Saturday night, maybe some travelers, though this franchise is miles from I-59. Alex gives a closer look around only after he has ordered his chicken sandwich and onion rings, Henry's fries. There are no teenagers, only two kids who look Henry's age, maybe a bit older, throwing fries at each other in a booth.

"To go," he tells the cashier, an older woman with a pleasant glued-on smile that reassures Alex.

"To go?" Henry asks.

"I don't want to eat here."

Henry accepts this with a shrug, and Alex fidgets while he waits for his order to be bagged and handed over.

And then they come in: his former friends, Tyler and Kirk. He knew this would happen, maybe he even hoped for it to happen: to run into his old friends, to see them away from school, and for them to see him. *Them*—they have become a collective unit in his mind.

With these two here, Alex thinks that the girls can't be far behind, some of the other guys too. A group of about ten of them, a real adolescent gang. Decreased in number now by one. Alex watches as they walk in, their eyes up at the glowing menu, so they haven't noticed him yet. Alex looks away, anywhere but where the boys are. The cashier scoops his onion rings. The drive-through alert beeps, and one of the cooks shouts something to someone farther back in the kitchen.

"Alex." A young man's voice, Tyler's.

Alex turns and Tyler lets out a tiny wave, almost just a hand raise, nothing more. "Oh, hey," Alex says. Kirk nods. Alex notices for the first time how similar these two look; they could be twins—brown hair, left long and kept intentionally messy, black-brown eyes, shave-burned necks, trimmed sideburns, jeans with plaid shirts tucked in, leather hiking boots with jeans tucked into them. Alex, luckily, took off the robe before coming in the store, but he's sure he looks absurd to them anyway, in sneakers and loose jeans, his thin corny T-shirt, especially when it's so cold outside.

"How's it going?" Tyler asks.

"Fine." Alex looks down at Henry. "Just grabbing some food."

"Cool."

The woman hands Alex his bag, smiles at him, and moves to take Tyler and Kirk's order.

"It was good seeing you," Tyler says, ignoring the cashier, and for a brief moment Alex thinks Tyler's about to say something more, ask him to stay, sit down, join them, call him later, something. But he looks at Kirk and says, "You ready to order? Go ahead." Kirk, who hasn't bothered speaking to Alex.

Alex motions for Henry, who Kirk and Tyler seem not to have noticed. "Bye," Alex says.

"Bye," they both murmur, Tyler giving him one last quick glance, Kirk scrutinizing the menu as if he hadn't eaten there a million times before.

At the door Alex pauses and hears Kirk snicker, say something under his breath, and Tyler joins in and snorts out a laugh, and right then Alex pushes open the door and enters the coldness and the twilight.

In the car, Henry munches on a french fry and asks, "Who were those boys?"

"Nobody."

"Okay."

"They were my friends."

"Okay."

Back home, after eating his food straight from the bag, Alex stretches out on the couch, wearing his shoes. Henry stands by the window. It's dark outside and lights are popping on in the neighboring homes, but no lights are on in Alex's house.

"Your mom home yet?" Alex asks.

Henry just shakes his head side to side and sniffles.

Alex sits up and looks at Henry. He listens as Henry begins to sob, his body shaking, his hands held over his ears as if he is trying to block out the sound of a loud siren. The vodka—which he resumed drinking once he got home—has made Alex feel tired, but he stands up and walks over to the window. "Don't," he pleads. "Henry," Alex says, touching him on the shoulder. He takes a deep breath. "Stop." But he keeps going, a near-silent cry. "Henry? I think it would be kind of okay if you stayed here tonight. If you want. Until your mom gets back."

Henry, like a wind-up toy slowing down, stops shaking and looks up at Alex. Although it's dark in the house, Alex can see his wet, blank face, the tears streaking it like little inlets of salt water. Henry rubs his eyes with his fingers, sniffles, and, struggling to catch his breath, says, "Okay."

Alex has left Henry in the living room and carried the bottle of Mr. Clean back to his parents' bathroom. He opens the cap and sniffs around the edges of the bottle and the ammonia smell tickles his nostrils. Henry knocks on the door.

"What are you doing in there?" he asks from outside.

Alex pours the bottle out into the sink and runs his fingers over the sticky remains on the ceramic basin and listens to the liquid escape down the drain.

"Alex?"

"Just cleaning up," Alex says, too quietly for Henry to hear.

"What?"

"I'll be out in a minute."

"What'd you say?"

Alex hears him shake the doorknob. This time he was careful to lock the door, though now that doesn't matter. He puts the cleaning fluid back under the sink, and he knows his mother will eventually see that it is empty and probably suffer a moment of fear. But then she'll find Alex, sitting reading a book or watching TV, not passed out on the floor, and her fear will subside, though it might never disappear, not for a while. Alex knows he may never be trusted again, but here he is alone—well, mostly alone—and he's fine. Drunk, but fine. They'll see that, they all will. Henry stops jiggling the knob. But then Alex opens the door and sees him there, almost panicked looking. "Okay, okay," he says.

"Sorry."

"No, it's okay," Alex says. "It really is."

At midnight the two boys sit at the kitchen table drinking hot milk, because Henry said it's what people in the movies drink to help them sleep. They have put sleeping bags on the living room floor, but they aren't tired yet. The dictionary lies open on the table and Henry thumbs through the thin, tissuelike pages, reading definitions aloud. And soon they hear a car pull up outside, and then the engine stops, but it's hard to tell where the sound of the car is coming from—it could be from one of the houses next door, or from the driveway of Alex's house, or even from Henry's garage. It could be James, or Henry's mother, or just a neighbor returning home late from a party. Maybe even Alex's parents, returned early. When they hear a car door slam, they both look up at each other, listening, but they don't rush to the window to see who it is. They stay seated, continue with the dictionary, and wait for whatever will happen next, even if nothing happens at all, even if they continue to sit there with their milk and words and each other.

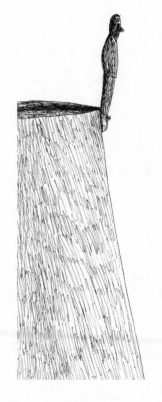

On the Brink

PASCAL LEMAITRE

About the Contributors

GREGORY GALLOWAY is the author of the novel *As Simple as Snow* (Putnam). He has an MFA from the Iowa Writers' Workshop and lives in New Jersey.

TABITHA SOREN spent ten years working on the air at MTV but is now a professional photographer whose work has been exhibited at galleries in Northern California and at the Oakland Museum. She lives in the San Francisco Bay area.

SHARON G. FLAKE won the Coretta Scott King/John Steptoe Award for New Talent with her first novel, *The Skin I'm In* (Jump at the Sun/Hyperion). Her second novel, *Money Hungry* (Jump at the Sun/Hyperion), was a Coretta Scott King Honor Book. She lives with her daughter in Pittsburgh.

KIWI, also known as Kirsten Smith, is a literary poet and a screenwriter who has written the films *Legally Blonde* and *Ten*

Things I Hate About You with her screenwriting partner Karen Lutz. Kiwi lives in Southern California.

DAVID LEVITHAN is the author of the novels *Are We There Yet?* (Knopf), *The Realm of Possibility* (Knopf), and *Boy Meets Boy* (Knopf), which won a Lambda Literary Award. Also the editor of the PUSH imprint at Scholastic, he lives in New Jersey.

MO WILLEMS spent nine years as a scriptwriter and animator for *Sesame Street.* Currently head writer for Cartoon Network's *Codename: Kids Next Door,* he is a six-time Emmy Award winner. He is also a two-time Caldecott Honor recipient for his acclaimed children's picture books. He lives in Brooklyn, New York, with his wife and daughter.

BENJAMIN M. FOSTER is a songwriter and musician who headed the seminal punk band Screeching Weasel as well as the Riverdales and, currently, Sweet Black and Blue. Writing as Ben Weasel, he is the author of *Like Hell* (Hope and Nonthings) and *Punk Is a Four-Letter Word* (Hope and Nonthings). He and his wife live in Oak Park, Illinois, where he is working on a new novel.

TERRY QUINN is the author of two novels, a biography, and a volume of poetry. He has also written the books, lyrics, and scores for three off-Broadway music theater works and the librettos for two operas. He lives in Brooklyn, New York.

MANUEL MUÑOZ is the author of *Zigzagger* (Northwestern University Press), a collection of short stories, and the recipient of an NEA fellowship for 2006. His work has appeared in many journals, including *Swink, Epoch,* and *Boston Review,* and has aired on National Public Radio's *Selected Shorts.* He lives in New York City, where he is at work on a novel. His second collection of short stories will be published in 2007 by Algonquin Books of Chapel Hill.

YANN MARTEL was born in Spain and grew up in Costa Rica, France, Mexico, and Canada, where he currently lives (when he's not living somewhere else). His internationally bestselling novel *Life of Pi* (Harcourt) won Britain's prestigious Man Booker Prize in 2002. His short story collection *The Facts Behind the Helsinki Roccamatios* (Harcourt) was published in the United States in 2004.

HELEN FROST, once a fifth-grade teacher in Alaska, is a poet and author of the acclaimed *Keesha's House* (Frances Foster/Farrar, Straus & Giroux), a Michael L. Printz Award Honor Book. Her other books include *Spinning Through the Universe* (Frances Foster/Farrar, Straus & Giroux) and the forthcoming *The Braid* (Frances Foster/Farrar, Straus & Giroux) which is excerpted in this issue. She lives in Indiana with her husband.

ELIZABETH E. WEIN, who has a PhD from the University of Pennsylvania, is the author of three acclaimed Arthurian novels: *The Winter Prince* (Puffin), *A Coalition of Lions* (Puffin), and *The Sunbird* (Viking). She lives with her husband and their two children in Scotland.

TOMMY KOVAC, an artist and graphic novelist, is the author of *Stitch* (Slave Labor Graphics) and *Skelebunnies* (Slave Labor Graphics). His latest creation, *Autumn* (Slave Labor Graphics), a mysterious and menacing story in eight issues, debuted in 2004. He lives in Southern California.

BENNETT MADISON attended Sarah Lawrence College. His first young adult novel, *Lulu Dark Can See Through Walls,* was published by Penguin Razorbill in 2005. He lives in Brooklyn, New York.

A. M. JENKINS was featured as a Flying Start author in *Publishers Weekly.* Her first novel, *Breaking Boxes,* received both a California Young Reader Medal and a Delacorte Press Prize for a First Young Adult Novel. Her second novel, *Damage* (HarperCollins), was short-listed for the *Los Angeles Times* Book Prize. She lives in Texas with her three sons.

MARTIN WILSON was born in Tuscaloosa, Alabama. He was educated at Vanderbilt University and the University of Florida. He lives in New York City, where he is at work on a novel.

PASCAL LEMAITRE is an internationally known artist whose editorial work appears in *Time,* the *New York Times, Le Monde,* and *Marie-France,* and elsewhere. He spends half the year in Brussels, where he teaches at La Cambre, and the other half in Brooklyn, New York, with his wife and daughter.

EDITORIAL ADVISORY BOARD: Frances Bradburn, Betty Carter, Aidan Chambers, Pam Spencer Holley, Jennifer Hubert, George Nicholson, Joel Shoemaker, and Deborah D. Taylor

About the Editor

Michael Cart is the author of the young adult novel *My Father's Scar* (Simon & Schuster) and editor of a number of award-winning anthologies. Former president of the Young Adult Library Services Association, he teaches young adult literature at UCLA and is the recipient of the 2000 Grolier Foundation Award for his production and promotion of outstanding literature for children and young adults. He appointed and chaired the task force that created the Michael L. Printz Award for excellence in young adult literature. Michael Cart lives in San Diego, California.

DON'T MISS

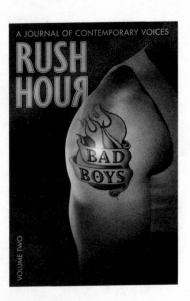